Femmes Fatale

Erik Scott de Bie

Amanda Cherry

CONTENTS

To everyone out there still battling their own demons

ROUND ONE: COCKTAIL HOUR

Vivienne Cain has made some questionable decisions in her life. She has a certain reputation for it, in fact.

The codename is low-hanging fruit. What possessed her to call herself "Lady Vengeance"—star of a number of demolished city blocks and seedy back alleys, a greater number of sexploitation graphic novels, and even more, even worse fanfics—she doesn't really know. At the time, it sounded cool and edgy and dark, very '90s, because, well, it was the '90s. Now, nearly thirty years after her debut as the formerly (and possibly still) demon-possessed anti-heroine du jour, the name sounds a bit like, at best, an outdated feminist statement, or at worst, a feminine hygiene joke.

Historically speaking, she has gleefully continued the trend of dodgy decisions. The black corset phase. Ripping out The Raven's eye. Getting involved with Marcus Orestes and her niece and their crazy. Carving her way into hell and back. Falling a little bit for Jaccob Stevens. *God.*

The decades of booze were probably a mistake, but at least they've been fun. Somewhat.

This, though.

This will be a mistake and not in a fun way.

"Ms. Cain? Miss Killingsworth is expecting you," the gender-ambiguous receptionist slash majordomo had said down in the extremely large and empty lobby.

"Miss?" Vivienne remembered murmuring.

Without another word, they gestured to a private elevator, and the light for "47" came on. The doors seemed to shut on their own, and she was on her way up.

Now, as the elevator whirs up the dizzying height of the skyscraper, Vivienne ponders exactly why she came here in the first place. Sure, she's here to confront (apparently *Miss*) Ruby Killingsworth, CEO of a major media empire. Seriously, with a name like that, how do people *not* assume she's a supervillain?

But *why*? What is she here to do?

Maybe she's here to fight. She flexes the silvery titanium-alloy claw on her left hand, imbued with demon-binding power and sporting nigh-unbreakable blades that extend four inches from each finger. Even just physically, it's a devastating weapon, like a cross between Freddy Krueger's glove and a Predator claw. It's something only some insane comics artist working in the extreme '90s would come up with, which she has always suspected is exactly what happened. The magic in the claw is the real threat, though. She knew that the moment she took it from a really creepy edgelord asshole who kidnapped and tried to use her to channel a demon lord to rule the world. Long story.

She still has the demon lord, of course, but he doesn't speak to her as often as in the old days. Thank God, Allah akbar, *inshallah.*

Aside from the claw, she also has her empathic projection. Since alcohol deadens her sensitivity to others' feelings and messes with the fear absorption, she hasn't had anything to drink today so her powers have a chance to work. (And it better be worth the raging headache.) She also spent the flight here absorbing a lot of fear—airplanes are good for that, especially on flights with lots of turbulence—until she's almost buzzing, like a cocaine or PCP high. She could smash through anything just now, especially some ginger tart named after a gemstone.

The elevator readout flickers through the twenties, picking up speed. Vivienne doesn't feel a lot of emotional energy in this place, suggesting it's mostly empty of people. It's also a relatively new structure, so it hasn't had time to collect the emotional resonance that builds up over decades. Across the plaza, Starcom Tower has its own resident atavistic spirit—one with *opinions*—but there's nothing here. The tower feels entirely under Killingsworth's iron control, and Vivienne's going to have to use what she's already got.

If this woman is half the sorceress Jaccob claimed, the fear energy will probably only go so far, but Vivienne has walked into and out of her fair share of ugly fights. From Jaccob's description, Killingsworth doesn't sound like much of a physical fighter, and a sober, fully prepared Vivienne can hold her own with the best martial artists in the world. Well, that was twenty years ago, but still.

Once she hits the thirtieth story and all the other buildings drop away, Vivienne sees the soaring edifice of Starcom Tower just across the plaza, and her heart leaps. Not that she finds compensation towers particularly impressive, but there's something about the place that just can't be separated from Jaccob "Stardust" Stevens, and thinking of him produces ... well, *feelings*. It isn't love, exactly, but something warm, intimate, and thoroughly outraged.

This woman hurt Jaccob—played with his heart for whatever reason—and she's Lady fucking Vengeance. If Stardust won't blast Miss Ruby Killingsworth into the next dimension, she sure as shit can.

Or maybe she's going up there to thank Ruby for teaching Jaccob a few things. About his heart. About magic. About the bedroom ...

Fuck.

Something happens when the elevator passes the forty-sixth floor. A shiver runs through her, but not a physical one—it's psychic. Something with real power. A magical barrier of some kind? It leaves her feeling shaky, even if she wasn't before.

God, this is a mistake. What the fuck is she doing here?

Too late.

The elevator dings, and the doors slide open to a sumptuous waiting room. Massive wrap-around windows offer an excellent view of Starcom Tower and Cobalt City beyond, though glittering automated drapes have covered most of them just at the moment, probably to block the glare of the afternoon sun. Where the walls aren't windows hang pictures of musical acts, award shows, and red-carpet walks of every possible variety. Trophies and awards in glass cases replace furniture in most of the lobby, but not quite as much as a museum—this is still a workspace.

She passes through the too-chic lobby, past a conference room with spotless glass walls, and down a hallway that could only be this long on purpose. The heavy double doors at the end are unmarked, but there's no question what lies on the other side. They might as well have "Oz, the Great and Powerful" emblazoned above the door frame.

The doors seem to open on their own, and Vivienne knows it's now or never. If she was going to turn back, she'd have done it by now. She does her best to feign confidence as she makes her way through the outer office—empty save for an assistant's desk that appears never to have seen a day's work—and through the open wooden doors into the main arena beyond. She steps inside the massive chamber, trying her best to take it all in without dropping her guard or letting herself get too off-kilter.

It's a challenge.

Everything here is curated to impress or intimidate, and if Vivienne were any weaker of constitution, it would probably work. Each of the fine, gleaming chairs looks more expensive than all the furniture in her bar and apartment combined. One massive desk dominates the space, no doubt sculpted of reclaimed wood or possibly salvaged from some ancient European castle. Either way, it's a pretty damn impressive piece of work, and Vivienne has the immediate urge to run her hands along its lacquered surface.

She'd have some trouble doing that, of course, what with the mountain of papers and pictures on the desk. And even at a brief glance, she can tell what they're about. The files have her name all over them and consist mostly of reports, evaluations, and quite a few printouts of newspaper stories. The pictures are of her, mostly, at various points in her career and at various levels of compromised propriety: a few indecent things well worthy of blackmail, not to mention stills of that leaked porn video she shot with The Valencian, where he made her wear the extra slutty costume with the underboob window, and she got him to dress up like The Raven. (Bad decisions, thy name is Vengeance.) The desk is, as a trashy police procedural would call it, a mountain of incriminating evidence.

And there, in the middle of the room, supervising it all like a green widow spider at the heart of her web, stands Ruby Killingsworth. Some evil masterminds would be sitting when the hero showed up, as a way to show their power and complete ease in the situation. Ruby, however, stands, turned halfway away as though interrupted in the middle of looking at one of the files on her desk, effortlessly comfortable with her space, decked out in a high-slit, emerald-green dress that flatters her long, perfectly styled, fire-red hair. She has the proportions and build of a 1950s bombshell, and Vivienne suddenly imagines her painted in almost that exact pose on the nose of a fat boy nuclear warhead. Maybe winking.

It really makes Vivienne feel underdressed, in her half-washed black jeans and beaten-up black leather jacket. Maybe she should have done something with her hair. Eh.

"Oh," Ruby says, feigning surprise and making it obvious. "Miss Cain, what a surprise. Come in, won't you?"

Ms., Vivienne thinks but doesn't say. She won't give her the satisfaction.

From Jaccob's stories, Vivienne expected someone of surpassing beauty, like a temptress you can't help but want at first sight, like Lauren Bacall out of a black-and-white noir detective movie, using magic to light her cigarette without a lighter. But aside from a vague stirring that she attributes to her weakness for redheads, Vivienne thinks Ruby Killingsworth looks, well, rather normal. Lovely, sure, in a stern, mature way. In charge. Actualized and in command of her own power. No one holds any chains over her. She's the empress of all she surveys. A woman not to be fucked with, and she knows it.

Which, of course, means Vivienne has to fuck with her. Call it a job requirement.

"You're her, huh?" Vivienne crosses her arms. "The other woman?"

"Well, who else would I be?" Ruby asks. "And I guess that makes you the *other*, other woman."

"Funny."

Unperturbed, Ruby crosses to the other side of the desk and sits in the finely upholstered administrator's throne. It's a proper Bond villain chair, at least: high-backed and probably bulletproof. There she sits, crossing her legs quite delicately, the slit in her dress revealing more leg than would qualify as demure. She doesn't quite smile, but Vivienne can tell she wants to. Oh, the woman is smug in the extreme. If Vivienne Googled "sneer," that exact expression would be one of the first image results.

Also—and Vivienne can't help but stiffen a little at this realization—there is absolutely nothing coming off her. No anger. No self-satisfied pride. Especially no fear.

Genocidal megalomaniacs are usually pretty angry, which tastes like burnt coffee, and manipulator supervillains usually give her righteousness with a faint aftertaste of deep-seated insecurity. Psychopaths still produce emotions, stunted and strange things with a different flavor from those of normal people. After nearly

5

thirty years in the life, Vivienne has met more than a few of those in her time, and slept with a few, too. Ruby Killingsworth isn't one of them.

Ruby Killingsworth is just blank.

There *is* something, though. The air around her chair ripples slightly, like a heat distortion Vivienne can taste rather than see. Magic of some kind, or ...

"I take it everything is working, then?" Ruby asks, savoring her triumph.

"Your protective spell? Yeah, I guess." Vivienne shrugs off her leather jacket, hangs it on the back of one of the chairs, and flops down, crossing her legs over the arm. She stretches languidly. "It's no big deal. I came armed for bear." She runs her fingers along the leather. "Ooh. Corinthian?"

"*Corinthian.*" If Ruby could knock herself unconscious rolling her eyes, she would do so now. "Moroccan, 18th century. Refurbished, obviously."

"Nice." Vivienne cracks the knuckles of her bare hand, one-handed. "So your spell blocks my powers. You having any luck pushing me on your end?"

"Not quite." Ruby's cool, in-control expression doesn't waver, but the edge of one eye twitches in a way both irritated and adorable. "I'll make the effort if I need to—but so far things have been perfectly civil. Why break a sweat when I don't have to? I think you already know everything you need to know about me."

"You mean that you're a witch? Yeah, Jaccob may have mentioned it."

"I prefer sorceress, or magic user."

"Oh, I'll bet you do."

"It's more acceptable in polite company. Though—" Ruby takes in Vivienne's look, from the thorn vine tattoos on her bare arms to the crescent hanging from the dog collar on her neck to the tight black t-shirt with the purple and white cartoon goth girl that says "bitch" at the bottom. "I'm not sure this qualifies."

"Oh, I'm hurt. Look how I am wounded." The distortion is becoming a little clearer, and Vivienne keeps her cool. Slowly, she traces the fingers of the claw through the air, writing purple runes of fire.

Ruby tenses slightly, but she doesn't raise an objection. She probably has contingencies for an attack.

6

"Look, maybe we should talk business?" Ruby asks. "Not that I don't appreciate this whole, leatherdyke thing you've got going on. Very retro. Just looking at you is making me want to play a hair band power ballad."

"Heh. Left my bike back in Seattle." Vivienne leans back, seemingly casual. "Jaccob didn't mention you were a, you know, fan of the Babadook."

"Outdated cultural references for 100. I'll have you know I am a genuine pansexual whose lovers have included men, women, mortals, gods, and several beings in between."

Vivienne smiles. "I prefer the term 'bisexual,' myself. I know, I know—old-fashioned."

Ruby returns that smile, full of teeth. "And exactly how old are you, dear?"

"Oh, fuck you, Ginger."

Through the banter, it's finally come into focus—the darkness swirling behind Ruby. When she first saw the distortion, Vivienne realized what she was dealing with, and while she's surprised to see the full scope, she knows what to do. Kind of derails her whole approach, but oh well.

"Well, I do know *one* thing you might find interesting," she says. "Sensed it when I came in, but it took all that stalling just to be sure."

"Oh?" Ruby looks on the verge of bursting a blood vessel. Maybe even her own. "And what's that?"

Casually, Vivienne gestures with the foretalon of her battle glove, pointing not at Ruby, but over her shoulder. "There's a demon standing right behind you."

"Oh?" Ruby scoffs.

Surely that's a bluff. And honestly, it's a little irritating. How typical.

As a child, the slightly awkward, socially despised girl who would become Ruby Killingsworth never got on too well on the playground or made a lot of friends, but she was always very good at one thing, and that was homework. It gave her important skills for the rest of her life—diligence, self-reliance, inquisitiveness— and they have served her well.

For instance: as soon as she saw the first paparazzi shots of Jaccob Stevens out and about in Seattle with his bad girl rebound, she set out to learn everything she possibly could about Vivienne

Cain, a.k.a. Lady Vengeance, semi-retired. She tasked her assistant with all the internet research, hired a Seattle-based PI to dig up some dirt, and personally put in some scrying legwork. Most of the information was at least ten years old, but there was plenty. The woman had a history and quite a few enemies, an impressive collection of whom had been more than happy to talk to Ruby. Emails to The_Raven@valhalla.gov had gone unanswered, but she found plenty of dirt from other sources. After a few divination rituals and deep dives into dusty tomes on semi-legitimate loan from the Cobalt City Archives, Ruby probably knew more about how Vivienne's powers functioned than the woman herself did.

Despite all the pictures, the files, and quite a bit of careful spell-work in preparation, Vivienne had stridden into Ruby's office as though she owned the building, seemingly unconcerned. All well and good. That amount of willpower, Ruby can respect. This is one of her places of power, and it takes an appealing level of guts to defy all that.

That, and her extremely lovely purple eyes, like a well-aged bottle of Bordeaux. Her slightly dark complexion, hinting at Middle Eastern heritage, her dark eyeshadow and lipstick somewhere between purple and black; it's a good look.

But then, to turn it all on something so obviously bogus? That's just insulting.

"Oh, darling," Ruby says. "What kind of an amateur do you think I am? Next I suppose you're going to tell me my shoe's untied. It's not going to work. Not even a little."

Vivienne raises her brow. "I get it. Pride. That's your thing, isn't it?"

Oh, that is *it*. "Look, I tried to be nice."

With a gesture, Ruby evokes the trap spell she prepared on the Moroccan leather seat, and Vivienne sits up straight as a rail, trapped by waves of force that crush her between them like two invisible mattresses. She got the idea from seeing a Stardust gadget, actually, which he gleefully described as two repulsor projectors pointed at each other. See? She listens.

Importantly, the force pushes Vivienne's gloved hand back out and to the side, the claws pointing harmlessly away from Ruby. She looks rather appealing that way, all trussed up in Ruby's magic like a puppet with its strings pulled tight in all directions.

8

"Come ... on ..." Vivienne manages against the force wedging her jaw mostly shut.

"Hush." Ruby reaches through the magic, which flows harmlessly over her hand like water, and strokes Vivienne's cheek. Then she half-pats, half-slaps her. "You tried, but you came in unprepared. Whereas—"

Abruptly she realizes Vivienne is using magic, and she frowns. It isn't some sort of attack—that would splash off her personal mantle like the tide breaking around a rock. Instead, she's drawing something in, rather than projecting it out. Metabolizing energy, but how? She can't drain Ruby for the same reason, and besides, the wards on the building should be blocking that. And she cleared every employee and resident out of the building hours ago.

Unless she can soak up Loki's power, but that isn't possible, is it?

"What are you doing?" Ruby asks. "Where are you taking power from?"

Vivienne's eyes have darkened and gleam with purple energy. "Just ... look ..."

"Fine." Ruby casts a spell of revealing with a few quick gestures and a flicker of will. "But I won't—"

She pulls up short and catches her breath.

There it is.

The creature is easily twelve feet tall and stick-thin, with a dozen spindly arms the color of tar, like a blackened birch tree crossed with some kind of long-legged spider. It stands behind her throne-like office chair, leaning two of its many hands on the desk, and looms over where she was sitting all morning. Its head has no clear human features but a series of hollow maws and branches ending in crimson marbles that might be eyes. As she looks at it, the head turns toward her, and several of its knothole mouths open, revealing yawning darkness.

Heart throbbing, she staggers back into Vivienne, whose arms wrap around her to steady her. The magic trap must have failed when the vision broke her concentration. Vivienne's embrace is surprisingly gentle.

"Is ... is this you?" Ruby asks, furious at how weak her voice sounds. She read about Lady Vengeance conjuring fear illusions, but this ... She never imagined something like *this*.

9

"I wish. That's a demon. Ramisiel, if I'm not mistaken. We've never met in person, but I know him by reputation. He's a whole gaggle of dicks."

"He *is* a gaggle, or—" Ruby eyes those protuberances she took for eyes. "—or he *has* a gaggle?"

"Well ... maybe don't let him grab you."

"Great."

Ramisiel seems to realize Ruby can see him—It? They? Vivienne called it a him—and lurches up from leaning against the desk. The demon's head twists slightly to the side, the way a cat might turn its head when looking in a mirror to see if its reflection will follow. His stalks wave in an unfelt wind, and Ruby realizes he's testing her perception. Maybe if she realized that earlier, she could have pretended not to see him. Ramisiel steps forward, three legs unfolding and jabbing into the floor.

"Hey," Vivienne says. "Stay calm. It's all right."

"Oh sure it is." Ruby tries not to focus on how strong Vivienne feels against her back. Not muscular, exactly—not like Jacob's washboard abs or that time she had the fling with that MMA fighter, *Gods*, she'd been hot—but strong. Hard. Determined. "What do we do?"

"Run."

"Wait, what?"

Before Ruby can react, she totters back on her five hundred-dollar heels as Vivienne drags her back toward her private elevator.

"Hey!" Ruby says. "What are you doing?"

A roar fills her office, and Ramisiel hurls the desk aside like it's a manila folder, sending the refurbished wood shattering against the wall in a shower of papers and photographs. Rage suffuses the floor of the tower, making the whole building shake. They dash through to the outer office and manage to make it to the elevator, while the demon creeps toward them, skittering forward on his many legs.

Come back, says a voice from somewhere. Ruby's never heard that voice before, but Vivienne seems to recognize it, and it makes her frown deeply. *Come back to me.*

Ruby's mind races for some sort of applicable magic, but she can't think of anything. Her limbs shake, and she can't make herself do anything but cower in the corner of the elevator as

Vivienne stands over her, rapidly tapping the button to close the doors. They don't respond.

"Oh, come on," Vivienne says.

"You need—" Ruby reaches her hand up to the palm print reader. "Try it now."

Vivienne presses the button for the lobby and watches as it lights up green.

The doors slide slowly shut, just as the demon looms over them. His limbs extend forward, and Ruby catches her breath, but the doors close just before it can reach inside. Ramisiel's touch bends the metal inward seemingly without effort, like human fingers shoving through damp paper, violent enough that Vivienne staggers back from the door, plastering herself against the glass opposite. She stands over Ruby, one arm protectively out, her clawed gauntlet thrust forward and gleaming with power. The creature roars in anger, making Ruby shake.

The elevator car screeches and shoots down the shaft, and Ruby blinks in shock at the dent in the door. Her ears ring from the creature's horrific shout.

She realizes Vivienne is saying something, but she can't follow it. "What?"

"Ok." Vivienne kneels to put the two of them face to face. "How many other employees in the building?"

"I ... I sent them all home. Only the building manager on the first floor. Security guards. For ... for you. Warded so you can't absorb their fears."

"Smart." Vivienne holds out Ruby's phone. "Call your building manager. Get everyone else out of the building. If you prepared for me, then I assume Ramisiel is trapped here?"

"On that floor. I've ... never summoned a demon, but I know the theory. I drew a circle to trap you, just in case—"

"In case I demoned out. Yeah." Vivienne looks so calm, but for the first time, Ruby realizes her shoulders are heaving and her hands are shaking. She's just as scared as Ruby herself, and that's comforting. "You're ... you're ok. It's ok."

"Wait." Ruby grasps Vivienne's bare hand, drawing her red-wine eyes to meet hers. "You're ok, too."

Vivienne starts to say something—probably something smart-ass—but the words won't come out. Something powerful flares between the two women, something that has been simmering since

11

they first laid eyes upon one another. Ruby feels it, and she's sure Vivienne does, too. Vivienne squeezes Ruby's hand back and runs her thumb over the back of Ruby's knuckles.

"This," Vivienne says. "This is a fucking terrible idea."

"Damn right it is."

Then they kiss.

Vivienne's lips are warm and taste of autumn and fine scotch. A shiver passes through her body, and Ruby can feel her heart beating fast. Against her, Vivienne's body is hard and firm, like a coiled spring, but she relaxes into the kiss, infusing it with all that pent-up energy.

The elevator dings and they draw apart, though neither really wants to. The door opens, clanking and grinding because of the dent in the metal, and Ruby looks up to see Arsho, their face stoic as ever, looking into the guest elevator from the first floor lobby. What they see there, two frazzled women entwined on the floor of the car, is worthy of a quizzical expression.

"Um," Vivienne says.

"Thank you, Arsho." Ruby reaches up and hits a button.

The doors slowly grind close, screeching in protest.

When they're alone in the elevator again, Ruby meets Vivienne's speculative purple gaze. Her lips are curled slightly in a way she finds both insolent and wildly attractive.

"If you tell anyone about this," Ruby says, "I will destroy you, emo girl."

"Same to you, Ginger."

They kiss again. Longer.

INTERLUDE: REFILL

Vivienne groans at the sound of the knock at the door. She didn't take this for the sort of hotel where the staff would harass her over not wanting fresh towels. "The sign says 'DO NOT DISTURB!'" she shouts, and immediately regrets that decision. She wanted all her wits about her and every bit of power available when she went to meet Jaccob's ex in her office, and so had gone in with nary a drop of liquor in her system. But that level of sobriety had never suited Vivienne well, and the unpleasant side effects of such, along with the memory of some ill-advised kisses in the elevator, had sent her careening from the Ruby Tower and into a corner seat at the nearest bar. She'd stayed there until a kindly barback had poured her into a cab back to her hotel.

She has no idea what time it is, nor how long she's been passed out. She also has no idea what became of most of her clothes. But what she does know is that she has a splitting headache and no desire for company.

The knock sounds again.

"Go away!" Vivienne calls back.

"Let me in, Vengeance."

"Fuck."

Before yesterday, Vivienne had never heard that voice, but now she would know it anywhere. She rolls out of bed and stumbles to the door, tossing on shirt as she goes, but not bothering with pants. She knocks the swing bar aside and turns the handle just enough to release the bolt.

Vivienne is barely able to clear the entryway before the door swings fully open to allow Ruby Killingsworth to step inside. She looks good. Too good. She's wearing a white tailored pantsuit with a magenta blouse that shouldn't work with her hair color and yet somehow does. Her hair is down, loose, and shiny, and whatever perfume she has on smells so good it ought to be illegal. The damn woman is every bit the image of polish and perfection—from the top of her head to the tips of her obscenely expensive shoes. No one should be able to look so damned flawless, especially at ... whatever time of the morning it is.

Vivienne lets out a grumble as she flops down to sit on the rumpled covers at the foot of her bed. "How the—" she begins, but the words come out as a mumble. She shakes her head and tries again. "Never mind. Of course you knew where I was staying. What was I thinking? So how about we start with what the hell you're doing here?"

"I need you," Ruby replies flatly. She is pointedly not looking at Vivienne's bare legs.

"Wow." Vivienne sits up a little straighter. She likes the sound of that, but it can't be all that's happening. She plays along. "That's a little forward—even for me. But you did look mighty hot in that little green number yesterday." Vivienne runs her hands through her still sleep-tousled hair, hoping it makes her look disheveled and fetching instead of unkempt and slovenly. She grins impishly, in spite of her headache. "I can't say I'm against the idea."

"While that's not at all what I meant when I said that—" Ruby tilts her head as she smiles back. "I'm absolutely game if you are. That is, after I have your help with my current situation."

"Current situation?" Vivienne can't help but sigh. From what Jaccob had been willing to share, Ruby Killingsworth has a *lot* of "situations," some of which Vivienne would just as soon have nothing to do with.

"You remember that demon in my office?"

"Sounds familiar," Vivienne replies, "might have heard of it."

"You're cute."

"So I've been told."

"But I digress. There is a demon in my building, and I'm going to need your help to get rid of it."

"You want me to help you with the demon? I'm not an exorcist. Pretty sure I said."

"I don't need an exorcist. But I do need help." Ruby's tone is hard, annoyed, and impatient. "I know where it came from, I know how it got here, and I know how to send it back. But I can't do it

14

on my own, and the sonofabitch it followed through the Coil to our dimension refuses to help—"

"You mean Loki."

Ruby's mouth falls open, then she purses her lips closed. It's more of a tell than Vivienne expected from her. And it's more than enough to confirm her suspicion.

"As I said, he refuses to help, says it's not his problem."

"I'm not so experienced with Loki myself, but that does sound about the right speed."

"Oh, it's entirely on brand." Ruby is frowning.

Vivienne takes note. She's beginning to suspect Ruby's acquaintance with the trickster god is more than a passing one. She wonders if this might prove useful.

"He says I can deal with it myself—and maybe I can. But demons aren't at all in my wheelhouse. And since you seem to know a thing or three, I figure you're my best choice."

"I'm not saying I'll help you," Vivienne replies, still taking stock of what Ruby had just revealed about her relationship with Loki. "But what do you have in mind, exactly?"

"We lure it down to a retail space." Every vestige of upset has vanished from Ruby's tone. She's all business now, matter-of-fact. At the same time, she crosses her arms over her chest and leans back against the dresser—body language that says she's at ease in the moment, confident in what she's about to say. The woman is a walking contradiction, and Vivienne is intrigued. "I'll make sure it's nice and crowded. Then you make it visible—the demon. Presto: all you can eat terror buffet. You use their fear to give you the power you need to go up against it. You'll get it distracted while I open a portal through the Coil to someplace better suited for a slithering cock monster. You chase it through, I close the portal, and then you and I are in the penthouse sipping cocktails before the insurance adjuster arrives to assess the damage."

"I thought you said you'd sent everyone home," Vivienne says.

"I did. I got Arsho to make up some bogus story about the wiring. Bonus that it puts in doubt the job Starcom did on all my installs. And anyway, I didn't necessarily mean my retail store. I was thinking more, we ought to lure it into Starcom Tower. That way, whatever the fallout, it's Jaccob's problem."

Heh. "As hilarious as that would be, there's no guarantee Ramisiel will leave your office, much less the tower, no matter how nicely you ask."

Unless ... but no, she dismisses that plan immediately.

"Drat," Ruby says. "Well, that is why we have insurance, isn't it?"

Ruthless, but maybe that would work. Vivienne takes in a deep but shaky breath. It's an awfully specific plan, but it has merit; no wonder Ruby seems so confident about it. Vivienne doesn't bother to wonder how Ruby knew about her ability to process the fear around her into usable power, but she does wonder something.

"You don't want to kill it?" she asks, pointing out what she thought was a more obvious method of disposition.

Ruby frowns. "I'm not sure I'd know how to kill it," she says bluntly. "And even if I did, I wouldn't have the first idea what to do about a demon corpse cluttering my office."

"But you're sure you can open a portal through the Coil?"

"Yes."

"How sure?"

"Certain." Ruby stands up straight again and steeples her fingers at her waist. "I'm sure Jaccob has already told you this, so it's not like I'm sharing any personal information here, but I went through a bit of an ordeal last year. It was like I didn't have any powers at all. And even then, I could open a portal through the Coil."

"Really?"

"Know-how trumps talent every day of the week. That's why I came to you for help. Maybe I have the power to dispatch this thing by myself, but I don't *know how*. And this isn't the kind of thing I care to learn through trial and error. You were able to see the demon, you were able to recognize it—knew its name—and you even shared some ... disturbing salient physiological details. I think you're just the person to help me get rid of it."

"Don't take this the wrong way—" Vivienne shifts in her seat and tries not to get distracted by the glint of Ruby's lip gloss. "—but why should I help you? And don't say it's because we kissed. I've kissed a lot of people, and I've never owed any of them a damn thing—much less demon hunting services."

"That's a fair question." Ruby is smiling with her eyes but not her mouth. Vivienne wonders what she's up to. "So, I'll ask one in reply. What will it take to convince you? Name your price."

"Seriously?" Vivienne's mouth is dry. She tries not to fidget. She can't decide whether this is a trap.

"Seriously. Anything you want," Ruby says blithely, "within reason."

"Right," Vivienne says, sure now it must be a trap, but somehow still intrigued. "And what is the going rate for 'reason' in billionaire circles these days?"

Ruby rolls her eyes and chuckles. She's shaking her head as she walks to the chair by the hotel window and lowers herself imperiously into it. She reclines just enough to easily prop her feet up on the corner of the bed.

It's weird to see such a classy woman put her shoes on the bed, but upon inspection of the pristine red soles, she forgets what she was going to say about it. Vivienne is at once annoyed and mesmerized, and she keeps mum.

"You can't have my business, or my building—and nothing of *sentimental* value is on the table."

"You mean magical artifacts. Grimoires. Cosmic evil kitsch."

"Mostly."

No surprises there. That's ok. In her experience, magic items are often more trouble than they're worth. She wonders if she should have put her claw on before answering the door.

"How about cash?" Vivienne asks then. She isn't sure how she feels about charging a fee for helping exorcise a demon, but Miss Killingsworth's answer will be a pretty good indicator of just how badly she wants this help. Vivienne wants that data point.

"Oh, that you can have," Ruby answers flippantly. "How much are we talking about?"

"Seriously?" Vivienne frowns. An infusion of capital could surely do her some good at the moment. And she has no reason at all not to take this insanely wealthy, unnaturally well-coiffed woman for a few dollars. What the hell. "Fifty grand."

It's a ridiculous number—just how ridiculous would remain to be seen. But Vivienne has nothing to lose. If Ruby calls it ridiculous and storms out, then so be it. The last thing Vivienne needs is to be getting tangled up with a billionaire sorceress, anyway. Isn't it?

But Ruby Killingsworth doesn't miss a beat. She slides a StarPhone from her pocket and starts to type.

"Do you know your SWIFT Code off hand?" she asks, as though that's the kind of thing a normal person would know. "Or would you prefer StarPal? I'll warn you—" She looks up over her phone at Vivienne. "—if you want *actual cash*, that's going to take a few days."

Unsure why, Vivienne springs from her seat. She's shaking her head as she crosses toward Ruby, only momentarily aware she's wearing nothing but a t-shirt and panties. "No. No ... really. That was just a ... don't ... really. No."

"Dammit, Vengeance." Ruby shoves her phone back into her pocket. She stands up to look Vivienne in the eye. "If you don't want money, then what do you want?"

"I don't know yet." Vivienne answers before she's able to stop herself. "Depends on how hard it is to get the job done. I'll tell you after."

Fuck.

The words left her mouth before she had a moment to think about what she was saying. Did she really just volunteer to help Jaccob's ex with a demon problem? What, because she's hot? Goddamn.

Ruby Killingsworth is all smiles. She's looking Vivienne squarely in the eye. It's a bit unsettling.

"It's a one-time payment," Ruby says, in a tone Vivienne can't quite place, "and you'll have ten days to tell me what I owe. I'm not going to spend the rest of my life ambiguously indebted."

"Whatever I want," Vivienne re-states. Her mind is already spinning with the possibilities—what she might take from this wicked sorceress and how she might use this opportunity to her advantage. "You promise?"

"I don't like promises," Ruby snaps. "In my experience, a promise is nothing more than a setup for disappointment. But I do make deals. And a person doesn't get to where I am in life if they can't keep up their end of a bargain."

"All right, we have a deal."

A burst of ice-cold air erupts between them then, and a crackle tickles at Vivienne's fingertips like a shock from a doorknob, a hint of cinnamon brushes against her palate. There's magic in this deal. Of course there is. She already regrets it.

"So." Vivienne scoots back to sit on the little hotel desk. She's trying not to let on that just having entered a magical contract with a ruthless sorceress has her nerves suddenly on edge, and she's not sure it's working. "Are we going to do this now, or—?"

"Day after tomorrow," Ruby declares, not waiting for any more of the question. "I think I'll have some autographs hidden in the store and put news of that out on social media. We want the biggest crowd possible for you to draw fear from."

Vivienne swallows hard, but nods. It's a good point. Any regular retail crowd should be enough to give Lady Vengeance what she'd need, but this was definitely an instance of "the more the merrier."

"There's just one problem with that," Vivienne says, doing her level best not to stare at the very pert, silk-clad DD-cups right at her current eye level. "I fly back to Seattle tomorrow."

"Well, now, it looks like you're going to miss your plane." Ruby says it like there was never any question.

There *are* questions, but Ruby is not staying to hear them. Before Vivienne can reply, she's on her feet and turns to go, a waft of that delicious perfume hanging in the air behind her.

"It's a non-refundable ticket. And the room is pre-paid—I have to be out tomorrow."

"Consider this little agreement to be travel expenses included," Ruby says without looking back. She turns the door handle and adds, "I'll have a car here in the morning."

Apparently, this conversation is over whether Vivienne wants it to be or not.

"And I'm just supposed to trust you?"

"We made a pact, did we not?" Ruby pauses in the doorway. She looks back now, at Vivienne, still sitting on the desk. "Just remember: my plan is sound, and my pockets are deep. I'll see you in the morning. Or I won't."

And then Ruby Killingsworth is gone.

And Vivienne Cain is once again alone with her headache.

19

ROUND TWO: APERITIF

Vivienne feels herself stumbling. The bottomless mimosas were only the beginning of the morning's bad decisions. But she needs the bulwark. She agreed to this, and she doesn't want to be called a liar—not by the likes of Jaccob's evil ex, anyway. But she'll be damned if she walks into that woman's limousine sober.

She spots the car easily: the slightly stretched Bentley Mulsanne stands out in the crowd of yellow cabs and family sedans. It might just cost more than this whole damned hotel.

Vivienne turns back for a moment—maybe one more drink to soothe her nerves, maybe one more shot at changing her mind.

"No," she whispers, sure she's already more than worn out her welcome at the all-you-can-drink mimosa bar. "You can fucking do this." Better to go through with it than to break a magical contract, she figures.

Calmly, with as much bodily control as she can muster, she makes her way toward the ostentatious automobile. If she still had any doubts as to whether it was the right car, the man who gets out to open the door for her quiets the last of them.

She will be getting into this crazy witch's car and going ... somewhere.

At least it's likely to be someplace posh. Maybe someplace with a good happy hour. She can only hope.

Vivienne allows the driver to take her bag from her shoulder as she ducks into the limo. And feels the whole of her guts lurch when she spots the crazy witch herself sitting on the opposite bench.

Ruby's wearing a blue suit that would have been boring on anyone else, but the deep V of the blazer paired with the sheer

21

nude blouse underneath speaks to one of Vivienne's more powerful fetishes.

This is going to be some limo ride.

"You're late, Vengeance." Ruby has a computer on her lap, and she doesn't so much as glance up from the screen as Vivienne climbs inside. "And drunk," she adds, still not missing a beat. "Is this again or still?"

Vivienne swallows hard. She feels judged and she doesn't like it. Worst of all is how much she doesn't like that she doesn't like it.

"I wasn't expecting you to be here." She tries and fails to avoid a sharp intake of breath when the driver shuts the door, firmly, right by her ear.

"It's my car," Ruby says, still not looking up from her screen.

"I ... get that." Vivienne tries not to slur her words. Had she known she would have company, she might have stopped drinking an hour ago. "But it's also one o'clock in the afternoon on a weekday. I figured you'd be working."

"There's a demon in my office."

"Right." Vivienne nods. She knew that. That's the whole reason they're in this car. "Still," she adds with as nonchalant a shrug as she can manage, "I didn't think I'd have executive escort for changing hotels."

"I wanted to be here to instruct the driver in case you decided not to show." Ruby quirks an eyebrow and switches which ankle is crossed over which. "And you're not going to any hotel."

"What?" This day was going to be a pain in her ass no matter what, but she didn't mentally prepare herself for being so puzzled so soon.

Ruby sighs audibly. Vivienne is sure her confusion is visible, or would be, were Ruby to bother to look at her. The lack of eye contact is unsettling. Vivienne doesn't like this feeling. She wants Ruby's attention, and it makes her uncomfortable just how strongly she wants it.

"Every time a member of my staff makes a reservation," Ruby says, still typing, "there's some reporter who thinks it's their job to investigate. And since we need tomorrow's operation to look spontaneous—and *not* like I lured a bunch of unsuspecting peasants into a music store to be fear fodder for a demon hunt—I figured it was better that you stay with me."

Nope.

"In a demon-infested building?" The car is moving now, but if that's the plan, Vivienne might just jump out the window anyway.

"No." Ruby finally looks up from her laptop. "We're not going to the Tower. I have a house in Regency Heights. We'll spend the night there."

"This feels like an awful lot of work to get me to spend the night with you." Vivienne is impressed at how cool her voice sounds. If she can flirt her way through this moment, she'll consider that a win.

"You and Jaccob Stevens!" The corners of Ruby's mouth turn upward in a way Vivienne finds equal parts alluring and infuriating. "You just presume any invitation back to my place means I'm trying to get into your drawers."

"Drawers?" Vivienne can't contain her chuckle. "Now there's a term you don't hear every day. Don't tell me you're secretly from Alabama."

"Louisiana, thankyouverymuch," Ruby snaps. "Born on a Bayou."

"That makes so much sense." Vivienne files that fact away in the back of her mind. She's studied numerous disciplines of magic and mysticism in her time, and she suspects Louisiana Voodoo might be a great place to start if she decides she truly wants to understand Ruby Killingsworth. Right now, she just wants to understand the plan for the next two days.

"Joke's on you," Vivienne says. "I don't even *wear* underwear."

Ruby looks at her dubiously. "Sweetie, I *saw you* in your underwear."

Oh yeah.

"Not that I object to shacking up with you—"

"In the same house," Ruby notes.

"Obviously that's what I meant." Vivienne rubs her temples. "But wouldn't it make more sense to do this today? I can kick Ramisiel's ass, get out of your hair, maybe even catch my flight. Easy."

Ruby blinks at her. "Bless. You think I can conjure a release party in under twelve hours. You don't even know what social media is, do you?"

"Hey. I know TeamApp. I've even used it, you know."

Ruby doesn't justify that with a response, but is that a tiny smile Vivienne detects? Maybe this is working after all.

23

Vivienne crosses her arms behind her head and leans back on the fine leather upholstery. "Anyway, it also makes sense to make tomorrow look spontaneous," she says, trying not to sound too impressed by this woman's scheming skills. Ruby is like seven steps ahead of her. "Which, I guess, makes the lodging decision a pretty practical one."

"And even if it wasn't, nobody gets to see the sex dungeon on their first visit."

"You have a—" Vivienne can't decide whether she feels shocked or titillated. But the look on Ruby's face tells her neither one is correct. "You're kidding."

"Am I?" Ruby's grin is as wicked as they come, the glistening cherry of her lip gloss drawing far too much of Vivienne's attention. "Truly, alas I have no dungeon," she says, but she doesn't leave it there. "I do, however, have a basement, to which you will not be invited, as well as no fewer than five guest rooms from which you are welcome to take your pick."

"So you're really not trying to get me into bed?" Vivienne isn't sure whether to feel relieved or disappointed.

"Really not."

Disappointed. Definitely.

"What if I want you to try?" Vivienne asks, instantly astounded how blatant she'd just been.

"How about we revisit this conversation after dinner?" Ruby grins again before turning her attention back to the computer in her lap.

~

"Dinner is served."

Vivienne looks up at the butler who's just called out to her. She has no idea what time it is or how long she's been in this room. She was shown here—to this lounge, or media room, or whatever this cavern was supposed to be—immediately upon arrival, with the vague instruction to make herself at home.

She did no such thing.

It's like a casino, this house. Bright lights, no clocks, and window shades that automatically lower and raise themselves to keep the sun in or out according to some arcane algorithm. The television was tuned to Entertainment News when she got here, and there's no making sense of the multitude of remote controls she might have used to change the channel. There's whiskey decanted on a table in the corner by the window—probably very good whiskey—but Vivienne decided sometime during the crosstown limo ride against adding additional liquor to her mimosa buzz. There isn't much she's been able to figure out about her current employer-cum-hostess for the night, but the one thing she's pretty damn sure of is that the more self-aware and in control a person is when dealing with her, the better.

It's been a long day, and a strange one, and Vivienne Cain is mostly sober, which is the strangest part.

Not, of course, that having that much willpower was a foregone conclusion. In this case, though, thinking about Ruby consumes all her mental energy, and she just hasn't felt like having a drink. Remarkable.

And it's dinner time.

Her stomach rumbles at the thought. Yeah. She's hungry. Dinner is good.

"You'll be joining Miss Killingsworth in the small dining room," the butler says. "Would you like me to show you the way?"

"Um, yes." Vivienne gets to her feet as he's turning to go. She's going to need to step lightly if she wants to get where she's going. There's no telling how long a person could remain lost in a house this size, but it would be entirely too easy to start.

It only takes a moment for her to catch up, because of the butlers she's encountered here, this one has the shortest stride. He isn't the same butler who greeted her upon arrival, nor the man who took her bag from the car and put it ... she really ought to find out where her things went. Including the claw—really convenient that Ruby stripped her of one of her most powerful weapons.

Hmm, Ruby stripping her ...

Focus, Vengeance.

If she'd known where her bag ended up, maybe she could have changed? It feels like this might be the kind of house where people dress for dinner. Not that she brought nice clothes, but she might have something in there a little less wrinkled.

She also wants to know just how many butlers one lady can employ. Because this seems excessive.

The whole *place* is excessive. What looks from the outside like a reasonable, if large, stone house, opens up in all directions to an interior the likes of which might have been cribbed from Versailles, or the damned Vatican.

Even going between the rooms that first butler said she'd have the run of felt a little like trespassing. She thinks that feeling could be magic. She wouldn't put it past Ruby Killingsworth to craft wards inside her ridiculous mansion to keep even the most welcome visitors from getting too comfortable.

Maybe it's all in her head, and she's just hungry and sober.

This butler looks younger than the others, handsome, too. She thinks about asking him if she ought to get changed, and where her bag is. He would probably tell her the truth.

But she decides she doesn't want to care. Who the hell is she trying to impress?

Fuck.

She pulls her shirttail up to her face, blotting it against her tongue before swiping underneath each eye, checking for marks of stray mascara and repeating the process until none are in evidence. She catches little glimpses of herself in the mirrors in the hallway. At least her face will look presentable—for certain values of presentable. She hasn't seen Ruby all afternoon, and she's about to. The handsome butler just told her so.

She doesn't like the butterflies her stomach gets when she thinks about seeing Ruby now.

In the last mirror before the stairs, she gives her eyes one more wipe and pats at her pockets for a lip gloss, which she fails to locate. She licks her lips, just because.

Vivienne follows the butler down a surprisingly long set of stairs, through a maze of rooms filled with books and pianos and artwork. The contents of any one room are probably worth more than everything Vivienne owns. She wants to hate this house, but somehow she can only marvel at it. Did Ruby instruct the butler to take her through every room in the house? *Nah.*

The butler stops at a doorway and gestures for Vivienne to go through it. "The small dining room, miss."

"It's *Ms.*, actually," she says. Or, she supposes, "Lady."

The butler nods and waits while she goes in.

"Small" is a matter of opinion, but it's the first room in this place that hasn't felt like either a storefront or a cave. It's almost homey in this room. Almost. It's honestly more like a display in a furniture store that's supposed to *look like* a home but doesn't quite hit the mark. Something smells good, though, like roast meat and browned butter, and that's enough to satisfy her for the moment. Ruby sits at a little table beside a window. She's changed her clothes. Wearing a black dress with a high collar and slightly puffed sleeves, with the front of her hair pinned up, she looks almost approachable.

Almost.

Vivienne reminds herself this is a business dinner.

She sits down across from Ruby, in front of a silver cloche and a too-extravagant place setting. Who has this shit in their house?

Yet another good-looking butler comes in and removes the heavy silver lids from the plates and vanishes through a door behind Ruby. That's four. She really is going to have to ask about that.

Vivienne looks down at the plate full of unfamiliar food; she thinks she recognizes a carrot, but it isn't the right color, so she can't be sure. Most disturbing, though, is what appears to be the main course.

"This is a tiny chicken." Vivienne tries to contain her level of alarm, but she's sure she's failing. "I mean ... I know you're evil and all, but you eat baby birds?"

"It's a pheasant, Vengeance," Ruby snaps.

"You eat peasants?"

"*Pheasant.*" Ruby shakes her head with a level of incredulousness Vivienne figures she probably deserves. "That's just the size they are. Think of it as nature's portion control."

Vivienne nods. Pheasant. That makes sense. She's made an ass of herself. About par for the course, as best she figures.

"Pheasant," she says quietly, picking up her knife and starting in on the diminutive fowl. "Portion control. *Tsch.*"

"I don't think the staff knew what to do with a single dinner guest," Ruby says then. She's pouring pale gold wine from a chilled decanter into a pair of crystal goblets Vivienne had guessed were just for decoration. "Usually I'm either here alone, in which case the menu is a handful of almonds and a wedge of parmesan, or it's some kind of dinner party featuring all five Young Dudes and everyone they've decided to invite to tag along."

"Is it true one of them is gay?" Vivienne's not good at small talk. Was that even an appropriate question?

27

"It is," Ruby answers casually, "although I won't tell you which one. And it's also true that Sturg Amondsen of Metalcholy works out all his chord progressions on a slide rule."

"He does?"

"Indeed." Ruby takes an almost obscenely languorous sip of wine. "Say what you will about heavy metal, but every one of his compositions is mathematically perfect."

Vivienne nods and goes back to eating the pheasant. It's tasty, as are the strangely purple carrots, and whatever this other vegetable is that's on her plate.

Ruby picks at her dinner. Vivienne thinks she should eat more but doesn't want to say anything. It seems like Ruby has something on her mind, but the silence isn't awkward yet. Vivienne finds that astounding and wonders how long it can last.

Ruby refills her wine glass and leans away from the table. Somehow her lipstick is still perfect; it's infuriating how flawless this woman can appear. Vivienne doesn't want to get caught looking; she tries to keep her eyes on her plate.

"This—" Ruby taps her red-polished nails against the crystal goblet in her hand. "I'm about to ask you an indelicate question." She takes a sip of her wine and then a deep breath. "The fact of the matter is I could just use magic to compel your answer but I'd really rather you just be honest with me. All right?"

Vivienne tries to say something, but her mouth is full of pheasant, and it only comes out as a grunt.

Ruby doesn't so much as pause. "I need to know about the drinking. Are you just a run-of-the-mill alcoholic, a party girl who can't help herself when she's out of town, or—as I strongly suspect—does it have something to do with your powers?"

Vivienne manages to swallow. When she looks up at Ruby, she's sure she looks like a deer in headlights.

"What—" she manages to ask. She reaches for the wine but stops short. Taking a swig from her water glass instead, she gets a hold of herself. "Where did you get that idea?"

Ruby sips her wine and sighs. Vivienne isn't sure if a reply is coming. But then Ruby leans forward, placing her elbows on the table. She holds up her wine in front of her face between steepled fingertips, looking at Vivienne carefully through the glass.

"Two days ago," she says softly, "you strode into my office as sober as a judge. Then, based on the condition I found you in yesterday morning, you likely spent every moment from the time we parted until I showed up at your door many, *many* sheets to the wind. And this morning when you got into my car, you were a good six mimosas in ... but you didn't expect me to be there. Since we've been alone in the house, you haven't touched a drop, even though there's been plenty available."

"You're not wrong," Vivienne mutters, but she doesn't mean to interrupt.

"I'm pretty close to the mark, aren't I?" Ruby seems rather pleased with herself. "When you think you need power, you sober yourself up; the rest of the time, you dull whatever senses you can manage." She sits back again, sipping her wine as she waits for a reply.

Vivienne only shakes her head as she goes in for another bite of pheasant. This isn't what she thinks of as acceptable dinner conversation. She wonders for a moment if maybe Jaccob tattled. But that couldn't be the case—she knows Jaccob and Ruby aren't speaking.

Fuck.

"It's not like I care," Ruby says. "Really, I doubt I could care less if I tried. You're an adult—use whatever substances suit you. Get as sloppy drunk as you please on your own time. It's just that we're about to go up against a demon tomorrow, and I need to know whether the difference between strong coffee and Irish coffee is going to have an effect on the outcome."

Vivienne dabs at her mouth with her napkin. She leans back in her chair. It's a fair question, if a personal one.

"It muffles the noise," she says after a pause.

"The noise is ... other people?"

"Yeah."

Vivienne takes a sip of wine and shrugs her shoulders. No need to keep this from Ruby, who seems to know a lot already, and the better equipped they are to work together, the sooner she can be done with demon hunting and back to Seattle, where she can hope to never hear the name Ruby Killingsworth again.

"You know how I can feel their fear, how I can use it?"

"Mm-hmmm." Ruby nods, sitting back from the table with her legs crossed, holding her wine glass, and hanging on Vivienne's every word.

"Well, what I can't do is turn it off."

"That sounds awful."

"It can be."

"And the alcohol dulls the sensation?" Ruby sets down her wine glass. Her gaze becomes intense. It reminds Vivienne of a cat sizing up a mouse before a pounce.

"That it does." That's not all, but she doesn't have to tell Ruby the other part ...

Faster than seems natural, Ruby is standing. She has the decanter in her hand and is topping off Vivienne's glass. "Is this enough, or should I send the staff home?"

"I'm good." Vivienne is stunned at the sudden bout of concern and for a moment isn't afraid to let that show. "But I'll drink this," she adds, picking up the very full glass from the table.

"Good." Ruby sounds satisfied. She fills her own glass and sits back down. "And I think you'll find I don't cause you much trouble in that regard."

Vivienne smiles. She feels a spate of honesty coming on. No harm in it now. "There's nothing." Then, more quietly: "Probably why I enjoy your company."

"I hope that's not the only reason," Ruby says over the rim of her wine glass. She takes a sip without breaking Vivienne's gaze. She's flirting now. Vivienne is sure of it.

"Nope, not the only reason." Vivienne flirts back. "But if it weren't for all that masking you do, I'm not sure I'd have noticed the rest. At least not right away."

"I keep my shit to myself, Vengeance. I have my own reasons. But I'm glad it makes this easier."

"You don't have to call me that, you know," Vivienne says.

"Would you prefer *Lady* Vengeance?" Ruby asks, her voice dripping with sarcasm. "I figured, after the way things went the day before yesterday, that we didn't need to stand on titles."

"Just V is fine," Vivienne says, unsure as to whether her sudden level of relaxation was coming from the wine, her full belly, some black magic, or the simple fact of having shared her truth with someone who hadn't given a damn beyond trying to make her comfortable.

"Are we already to diminutives?" Ruby asks. There's still sarcasm, but Vivienne can tell there's more behind the comment.

30

"Something like that ... Ginger." Vivienne quirks her lip. She wants another bite of dinner, but not as much as she wants to watch the gears in Ruby's head turn.

"I'll allow it," Ruby says after a beat. "But only in private. You're welcome to use my given name in public, although I'll warn you that's a tell—almost no one is allowed to do that. So if you'd rather not have people know there's something personal between us, it'll need to be Miss Killingsworth."

"Is there?" Vivienne asks then, working to get the last of her pheasant off its bones. "Something personal between us?"

"Well, I've let you into my office, my private elevator, and my crosstown residence. That's a lot more personal than I get with most people."

She didn't mention the kissing part, but why? Surely she doesn't just do that with most people. Unless she does? Vivienne feels herself starting to blush. It's not a feeling she welcomes. She casts her gaze quickly back at her nearly empty dinner plate and sees her escape there in the sauce-drizzled leavings.

"Portion control, my ass," Vivienne says, no longer caring so much about niceties. They've been being honest, no reason to stop now. "This was good, I want another one." She gestures to the picked-over pheasant bones on her plate and waits for her hostess's reply.

"Check the oven." Ruby pours herself what might be her eighth glass of wine. That's one hell of a decanter.

"Promise you're not going to push me in?" Vivienne hopes that came off as flirty, or maybe she doesn't. The only thing she's sure about is that she hopes there's really another roast pheasant someplace.

"Yes, yes, wicked witch and all that." Ruby's glass is full and her posture relaxed. "Do I look like I'm going to be getting off my ass anytime soon?"

Vivienne is sure she won't be. She smiles, rises with her empty plate, and heads to the door the butler made his exit through. Maybe she can at least find the oven without having to ask for directions.

Vivienne is pleased when the oven is immediately visible, on the far side of a kitchen larger than her apartment that looks as though no one has ever used it. Everything is white and gleaming; it's existentially terrifying in its tidiness. Also, there are two ovens,

31

which seems a lot for a person who never cooks and rarely even eats. But then Vivienne remembers tales of dinner parties past and starts back in on her pheasant hunting. The bottom oven is empty, but the top yields her promised quarry.

With no kitchen utensils in evidence, Vivienne grabs the fork from her plate and skewers one of the two birds still in the roasting pan. She plops the pheasant onto her plate, fork still attached, and bumps the oven door shut before dashing, rather indelicately, back to the table.

Ruby is still at the table. She sips wine as she reclines against the back of her chair. And Vivienne wonders what it might be like to be so put together.

Vivienne feels watched, like an animal in a zoo, but there's no telling the next time she'll get to eat a pheasant. And if Ruby Killingsworth feels the need to watch her eat it, then that's a small price to pay.

"That's a hell of a kitchen you got there," she says when the attention starts getting to her. She takes a sip of wine then blots her mouth with the ridiculous white linen napkin she found at her place when she sat down.

"If you think that's nice, wait until you see the rest of the house."

~

"And that's the music room," Ruby says, her voice evincing just the tiniest hint of a slur as she gestures with her wine glass at the door to the left.

"I thought I saw the music room downstairs. The one with the piano—" Vivienne points vaguely in the direction of downstairs "—and the other piano."

"One of them's a harpsichord. And that's the conservatory, actually."

"That's not the same thing?" Vivienne will never, ever understand rich people.

"Ground floor." Ruby turns to face Vivienne as she leans casually against the silk damask wallpaper. "Conservatory. Social space. Enough room for my guests and their guests to have whatever level hootenanny tickles their momentary fancy. Third floor, music room, just for me." She swirls her wine around in her glass and brings it to her lips. "One is for entertaining, and the other is reserved for my personal enjoyment."

"So I take it we won't be going in there." Vivienne's been challenging Ruby's boundaries since the first time their eyes met. Poking at the closed door to a private room was just another stage in the game.

Ruby smiles as she shakes her head. "I thought you might prefer to see this one." She gestures to a set of double doors just behind her.

"Oh?" Vivienne asks, mildly intrigued. "What's in there?"

Ruby grins. She reaches behind herself and turns the knob, swinging the door inward as she stands up straight and takes a single step backward.

"It's the master bedroom." Ruby turns and steps through the door. She casts a glance behind her. It's a "come-hither" if Vivienne has ever seen one.

Vivienne follows Ruby just to the other side of the threshold but keeps herself out of reach for the moment. Over the course of her life, bedrooms have been places in which Vivienne has made some of her most costly mistakes. And as much as she wants to fuck Ruby senseless, she isn't sure she's ready for what that means once they get back *outside* the bedroom.

This woman wrecked Jaccob. Is she really signing up for a taste of that destruction?

Silly question. *Obviously*.

Ruby stands stock still, both hands on her glass at her waist, her face expectant. That spider-waiting-to-pounce energy from the other day is back in spades.

Vivienne imagines a dozen ways to wipe that smirk off her face and starts ranking them in order of enjoyment.

For a moment, Vivienne's mind wanders to an imagined expression of ecstatic intensity, the idea of Ruby's mouth agape and her eyelids quivering in the throes of orgasmic rapture.

Self-destruction be damned. She's practically an expert by now.

She wants this, she's sure now. She takes a further step into the room. "Also for entertaining?"

"I'd say some of what's gone on in here has been very entertaining."

Ruby doesn't move; she's making Vivienne come to her. She's an accomplished predator, but Vivienne is no docile prey. She's willing to do the stalking if that's what's called for. She moves to stand close to Ruby. Too close. But not quite close *enough*.

"And your personal enjoyment?" Vivienne inches still closer, until their faces are barely a lip-width apart. She's committed to this now. Any voice in her head that might have warned her off getting into bed with Ruby, literally as well as figuratively, has gone silent.

"Oh." Ruby leans forward until their bodies are nearly as close as their faces. "That much is guaranteed." Ruby tilts her face upward just enough to brush her lips against Vivienne's.

Vivienne wants to lean in, grab this smug, imperious, infuriating woman by her impossibly shiny hair, and devour her right here on the blue plush carpet. But she won't.

There is power on the line here. These next few minutes could define their dynamic for good. And Vivienne refuses to be the needful one. She knows what's about to happen, and she's going to make the most of it. She is not about to chase Ruby Killingsworth, no matter how badly she wants to.

This game is just getting started.

"You sound so sure," Vivienne whispers, leaning away just so.

"Look around," Ruby says. "I know what I want, and I know how to get it."

Oh, this is excellent.

"And what do you want right now?" Vivienne tilts her head in a gesture of curiosity that should also make for easier kissing—real kissing—the kind that's to come just as soon as Ruby admits she wants it.

Ruby reaches over and threads her finger through a belt loop on Vivienne's jeans.

Vivienne feels her skin go prickly. She bites down on her lower lip as her eyes drift shut.

"You want me to tell you?" Ruby asks, with a light tug against the waist of V's pants. "Or do you want me to show you?"

Vivienne takes half a step back, standing up straight as she does. The force of her movement pulls Ruby off balance, and she stumbles forward, barely able to catch herself before running into Vivienne chest to chest. Finger still hooked through Vivienne's belt loop, Ruby lets her mouth come agape as she awaits her answer.

"I want to hear you say it."

"You first."

"Nuh-huh." Vivienne shakes her head.

Ruby pulls her hand away from Vivienne's waist. Both hands on her glass, she takes a step away. "Then I guess we're done here. Pity. Could've been fun. I'll see you in the morning." She moves to sip her wine as she turns to walk away.

Vivienne lunges, wine sloshing from her glass as she reaches to grab Ruby by her arm. Ruby snaps around again, wearing a snarl and with none of the previous moment's playfulness in evidence. Vivienne fears this is it.

It wouldn't be the first time stubbornness and power struggles fucked up her love life.

Sometimes she wonders if this is really her, or if it's someone— something else. The room becomes dark, or maybe it always was, because the two of them aren't alone in here. He's here, and no amount of drink will chase him away. Vivienne can feel him.

"Vengeance," someone says, and she's not sure if it's Ruby or *him*.

No. Vivienne drops Ruby's arm. Holding on right now isn't going to do anybody any good.

Ruby's frown intensifies. She turns again, and this time Vivienne lets her walk away.

"Power is a hell of a drug." Vivienne knocks back her wine and turns to go.

"The hell do you know about power?" Ruby asks as she rounds the corner of her enormous four-poster bed.

"I know you need to have it so bad you're shoo-ing a sure thing down the hallway, all because you won't be the one to admit you want it."

"All I said is you need to say it first." Ruby sets her glass on the ornate nightstand and sinks to sit on the edge of the bed.

"Because you won't say you want me until I've said I want you, because if you want something only I can give, then I have power over you, and you can't stand the thought of that." Vivienne takes another step into the room. She's looking Ruby in the eye as she crosses her arms over her chest. She's wrecked this already, might as well lay all her cards on the table.

"Oh, for pity's sake, Vengeance," Ruby says, picking up her glass again, "I didn't bring you here to psychoanalyze me." She keeps Vivienne's gaze locked in hers as she takes a leisurely sip of wine. "And also, you could not possibly be more wrong."

"Really?" Vivienne might not be able to feel Ruby's emotions through her protective spell, but she doesn't need her powers to read Ruby. She thinks.

"*Really*." Ruby's eyes show no sign of deception.

Vivienne doesn't believe her, but maybe she's misreading it. Maybe that little flash threw her off and she's making a fool of herself. She realizes she's sweating, just a little bit. Can Ruby tell? Probably.

She should really leave. Cut her losses, but ... dammit.

"Wanna tell me, then?" Vivienne asks. "If I'm not going to have a good time tonight, can I at least have an explanation?"

Ruby considers, then throws her head back and sighs. She drains the wine from the bottom of her glass and sets it back on the nightstand empty. When she turns back to Vivienne, she shakes her head, eyes rolling, and purses her lips a bit. "I need you to say it first," she says slowly, as though she were explaining a task to a child, "so that you'll remember you did."

"What?" Vivienne is shaking her head. She has no idea what that means. "Why?"

"So you'll know I didn't curse you." Ruby shakes her head again, but she's smiling now, wanly. "I didn't bewitch you, I didn't whisper a desire with a little too much intention behind it. I need you to say it first so you'll know—forever—that you did what *you* wanted, and not just what *I* wanted."

Vivienne realizes she's gaping, and she makes an effort to close her mouth. This wasn't a power game at all, but a power *check*. It isn't begging she wants, it's guidance. *Boundaries*. What she wants is a clear declaration of consent with no possible magical influence. Vivienne takes another step into the room, and another, slowly working her way toward where Ruby sits.

"You want to know my desires first, so you don't—"

"Magically fuck things up?" Ruby offers. "Influence your ability to withdraw consent? Yeah. So I don't, and you can be sure I didn't."

Vivienne closes the distance. She sets her own empty glass on the nightstand beside Ruby's and moves to sit in front of her on the bed.

"So if I say I want to go to bed with you," Vivienne begins.

"Then I can say: good," Ruby replies, relaxing a little as she does. "Because I want to go to bed with you. Specifics to be negotiated later."

"Really takes enthusiastic consent to a new level."

"V."

That. That single letter is enough.

Just like that, the oppressive presence is gone, and it's just the two of them, and the barrier is washed away like it was never there to begin with.

"Well," Vivienne says, "that's good, because I want to put my hands all over you."

They're communicating like goddamn adults, and somehow, it's a complete turn on.

"Is that so?" Ruby flicks her wrist through the air and the door to the bedroom abruptly closes. "Because I want to put my *mouth* all over you."

"That's good, because I—" Vivienne leans forward and props herself on her knee for a proper height advantage. "—have wanted to kiss you all day."

Ruby tilts her face toward Vivienne's. She reaches out to gently grab Vivienne by the neck. "So what are you waiting for now?"

Vivienne doesn't wait another moment. She leans forward to find Ruby's mouth with her own.

Ruby is all in now. She's done talking. She threads her fingers through Vivienne's hair, pulling her gently but insistently downward. She kicks her shoes off onto the carpet before wrapping her legs around Vivienne's, bringing their bodies closer together still.

They kiss each other harder. Vivienne runs her hand up Ruby's thigh, pausing only to marvel at the soft skin at the top of her stocking.

"Mmm, fancy." Vivienne nips at Ruby's ear as she snaps the elastic holding up the stocking hard against her leg. It's immediately apparent Ruby enjoys the sensation.

"I like nice things," Ruby whispers.

"You like naughty things," Vivienne counters, rubbing her finger over the warm spot on Ruby's thigh where the elastic made contact.

"You're damn right." Ruby runs her fingernails so roughly down Vivienne's back that she's almost grateful for the presence of her shirt. Almost.

"Good," Vivienne replies, still toying with the fascinating juncture of stocking and garter belt.

"Oh," Ruby says through a quickening breath, letting slip a little drawl, "it's gonna be."

And they're kissing again.

~

As rays of morning light peek through the small gap in the drapes, Ruby sits before the vanity in her bedroom, scrutinizing her contour from every angle.

Sorceress she may be, but makeup doesn't just *happen*—or at least, the spells that can make it just happen never get it quite right. And today she wants her face to be *right*. It takes another pass with the blending sponge for her to find herself acceptable. There's more she could do, she knows, but the look she's going for is as much "effortless" as it is "done." And the eyeshade she's chosen to coordinate with today's equally effortless outfit is a little darker than she'd usually do for daytime—a fact which may or may not have anything to do with …

"Murff," says the shape in the bed behind her.

Ruby shifts her gaze a little. The ring of light around the mirror is designed to fill this spot, and it casts interesting shadows into the room, particularly over the faint stirring in the bed. Vivienne is an awfully sound sleeper, but she'll have to wake sometime, and it's getting late. Hopefully she'll rouse before Ruby has to intervene.

Mornings after are always tricky, and often awkward, and this one has the added pressure of culminating in a demon hunt. So the last thing she wants to do is have to shake her big gun awake before she's ready.

Ruby shrugs and turns her attention back to her reflection. On her second cup of strong coffee and with her makeup only half done, she's not quite ready to face the day, much less her very attractive guest. A quick swipe of pomade through her perfectly threaded brows and she reaches for the setting powder. There. At least her face has a complete shape. Color will come in time.

She's vaguely aware as Vivienne rolls out of bed with a thump and tosses on the blue floral silk robe Ruby had left on her side of the bed. Good. She's up.

"There's coffee," Ruby says without turning around. Stealing glances in the mirror is one thing, but she's not about to give Vivienne her full attention.

At least not until her face is finished.

"Maybe in a minute," Vivienne says, her voice as groggy as the rest of her. Still, she smiles as she passes by, on her way into the master bathroom. "This fucking house," she grumbles as the lights come on automatically.

Ruby is pretty sure she wasn't supposed to hear that. She turns her attention back to the task at hand. It won't do to greet a lover with only half a face.

The water comes on, followed shortly by appealing swirls of steam. Was Vivienne born in a barn, she doesn't know to turn on the fan before she jumps in the shower? For a second, Ruby considers getting up to flick it on, but she's gripped with the overwhelming premonition that seeing Vivienne in the shower will tempt her into joining her, and then all her work of the morning will go to waste. Thus, she stays put, using magic to activate the fan instead.

The sidelong view in the bathroom mirror will simply have to do.

Well, all that research Ruby did on the woman, and she never realized Vivienne would have quite that many tattoos. It's really quite impressive—the ink, too.

Ruby is still sitting at her vanity, gaze fixed on her own reflection as she draws an impossibly narrow line across her upper eyelid, when Vivienne comes back, rubbing her mop of dark hair with one of Ruby's fluffy white towels. Her jaunty lean against the doorframe makes the silk robe she's wearing gape just so, and for a moment Ruby is tempted to stop what she's doing and have a closer look.

"I think your bathroom is bigger than my apartment," Vivienne says, stifling a yawn.

Ruby's gaze doesn't waver from her reflection, but she smirks a little, and shrugs. "That bathroom is larger than a lot of apartments." She picks up her china cup and takes a sip of coffee.

"And your tap water smells like lemongrass."

"Should I claim magic, or admit it's just a filter?"

Vivienne laughs once. It's partly the voice—that huskiness with a smooth whiskey finish—but Ruby likes Vivienne's laugh, too. "Toothbrush was a nice touch." Vivienne holds up a high-end toothbrush. Purple, naturally. "I almost expected it to be engraved."

"Glad you approve," Ruby replies, glancing sideways for a moment to grin at Vivienne before shifting focus to her other eye. "If you must know, I let a lot of my artists use the house when they're in town."

"You mean you didn't have one of your minions run out for personalized toiletries?"

Hrm. It simply wouldn't do for Vivienne to think there are spare toothbrushes around for overnight guests. It bugs her a little that she's concerned Vivienne might have formed that hypothesis, but she doesn't have time for self-analysis at the moment.

"Bless." Ruby leans back a little to inspect her handiwork. "I don't know how familiar you are with wealthy, famous boys in their twenties, but the ones of my acquaintance are prone to spontaneous sleepovers. So we keep a stash of hygiene supplies for use by the unsuspecting groupies. So no, I didn't get it specifically for you."

"Aw," Vivienne says. "And here I was, looking forward to picking out curtains."

"Funny," Ruby says with a smile. "As if I'd let you anywhere near my interior decorator."

"I do have my own toothbrush, you know." Vivienne eyes the mahogany tea cart at the foot of the bed. "It's with the rest of my things—in my bag, which your henchman saw fit to put somewhere safe yesterday."

"They're not henchmen, and they're not minions," Ruby says. "They're union."

"They're unbelievably attractive."

"I'm discerning."

"I see." Vivienne covers another yawn. "But you're changing the subject. My bag?"

Ruby takes another sip of coffee. She truly has no idea where Vivienne's things wound up. She didn't want to be so transparent as to have her bag brought straight to the master bedroom, and the thought hadn't dawned on her to make the request once the sleeping arrangements had been settled for good. She was ... otherwise occupied. "I'll have that brought up so you can get dressed. In the meantime, coffee."

This time it isn't an invitation. It's an insistence.

Vivienne nods in acquiescence. She's probably also noticed the lack of alcohol on offer. Ruby wants a fully loaded, sharp-as-possible Lady Vengeance for her mission. And Vivienne doesn't argue.

Strangely not awkward.

"I *do* like coffee." Vivienne pads across the plush carpet to the cart by the foot of the bed.

"I didn't know if you were a breakfast person," Ruby says as Vivienne pours her coffee. "If you need food, I can arrange for that. But we'll want to leave in less than an hour, so that will need to be handled sooner rather than later."

"No." Awkwardly, Vivienne picks up her coffee cup by its spindly handle. "But I could use a more substantial mug over here. I'm going to spill this."

"No, you're not," Ruby says, with a flick of her fingers in Vivienne's direction. She's able to catch Vivienne's expression changing when the cup becomes light and facile in her hand.

"You really had to magic my coffee?" Vivienne frowns, visibly unsure how she feels about the prospect of drinking from an enchanted cup.

"If it's that or risk a spill on my carpet, yes."

"It's probably really expensive carpet, too. I'll allow it." Vivienne walks back across the room to stand behind Ruby at her vanity. "That seems like a lot of work for demon hunting."

"Same as any other day." Carefully, Ruby dabs highlight beneath her perfectly arched brows.

"I want to be surprised that there is anyone on the planet who goes to this much effort every single day." Vivienne scrutinizes the sheer number of cosmetic implements on the vanity table, then shakes her head. "But on you, it just fits."

"I'm a public person, V. I require a public face."

"It still seems like a lot of work."

"Sometimes I can just use a glamour. But best not to be sustaining anything when I need to concentrate on a portal to elsewhere. Even a little distraction could throw the whole thing off." She captures her lashes in their curler, and Vivienne visibly winces as she pinches the pads closed.

"Wait a minute," Vivienne says. "Wait one goddamn minute." She steps around the vanity bench and wedges herself into the space left on the end. She finds Ruby's gaze in the mirror and glowers. "You made it sound like that portal would be no problem. You said you could do it with all your magic tied behind your back."

"Oh, I do like your metaphor." Ruby reaches for her mascara tube without breaking eye contact. Her lip quirks into a half-smile.

"We can talk more about tying things behind your back later," Vivienne says, "Right now, I want to go back to this portal thing, and how all of a sudden it sounds like a bigger deal than it did two days ago."

Ruby rolls her eyes before bringing the mascara wand to one set of sable lashes and then the other. "It's true that opening a portal is no more difficult than dialing a telephone. That is, for a person who knows how to work a telephone dial. Don't ask any of these nouveau wiccans to try it. But be assured, it is simple. Straightforward."

Vivienne is not assured, and it's all over her face. "Then why the 'no other magic' part?" she asks, finally sipping the coffee from her cup. "Why the 'best not be sustaining anything'?"

"Because there are unknowns," Ruby says coyly. She replaces the wand in the mascara tube and screws the lid shut before standing from her vanity stool and turning to face Vivienne, her gray silk dressing gown falling open to reveal the sheer lace nightie underneath. She looks good and she knows it. And if last night was any indication, Vivienne finds her particular brand of beauty quite alluring.

Ruby Killingsworth enjoys it when people look at her with lust in their eyes.

But it appears Vivienne is trying not to look at her at all. She's looking mostly at her own reflection as she absently plucks at the knots in her hair with her fingers. Does she even wear makeup, aside from that atrociously attractive lipstick? Ruby can't decide if she needs it.

"Do you want a turn?" Ruby asks primly.

"With your stuff? Pass. I don't even recognize half this stuff. So unless you've got—oh, here we go." Ruby watches, in no small amount of horror, as Vivienne picks out a dark eyeshadow and a lipstick essentially at random. "What are the unknowns?"

Ruby sips her coffee, a little miffed by the lack of attention, but still willing to answer the question—if only to get Vivienne to look at her.

"Unknowns." She starts toward the cart at the foot of the bed. "Like how big I'll need to grow this portal, how long I'll need to keep it open, whether I'm going to need to move it from here to there." She picks up the coffee pot and pauses, finally catching Vivienne's gaze. "How much energy I'm going to need to put into keeping the mortal nitwits from taking selfies with it."

"Selfies?" Vivienne is agog. "Selfies with a portal to a hell dimension?

"Oh yes. If there's one thing the last ten years in this business has taught me, it's to never underestimate the foolishness of a twenty-something with influencer aspirations."

"Yikes."

"My sentiments exactly."

"You know," Vivienne says, turning on the stool to face Ruby properly, "sometimes I think people our age just barely dodged a bullet. You couldn't pay me to be young in this decade."

"Cheers to that."

Ruby raises her coffee cup in the gesture of a toast. Vivienne toasts back. Ruby was expecting Vivienne's makeup to look garish, and it is very striking, but not in a bad way.

"So, these unknown factors," Vivienne says, putting the conversation back on track. "They can make holding the portal open more difficult?"

"Difficult isn't the word," Ruby says, waving her hand. "More like resource intensive. The more I have to do and the longer I have to do it, the weaker it could possibly get. And I don't want to be distracted by the fear of being photographed in my retail lobby looking anything less than my best. So I did this all the old fashioned way."

Ruby gestures vaguely with the coffee pot around her face and hair. How obvious does she have to be when she's fishing for compliments? Ugh.

"So what you're saying," Vivienne rises from her seat and heads toward the coffee cart where Ruby is still standing, "is that this whole getup—the perfect hair and flawless face—they make for better concentration, for stronger magic?"

Close enough. Ruby's mouth is full of coffee, but she nods. "Exactly," she says once she's swallowed. "It's practically a Fetish."

"Oh," Vivienne says, reaching out to take the coffee pot out of Ruby's hand. "Believe me, I want to hear all about all of your fetishes later today." She refills her cup before setting the pot back down on the cart. "But first we should toss a demon from a skyscraper."

"That's—that's it?" Ruby asks. "You don't need more prep time?"

"Like what?" Vivienne blinks. "I showered. I even washed my hair."

Ruby resists the urge to critique Vivienne's makeup choices, or to mention the fact she's failed to dry her hair. Oh, she resists, and it's harder than sustaining her will in conflict with certain evil artifacts. "No. Nothing. It's fine. Shall we?"

ROUND THREE: HAPPY HOUR

If someone had asked Vivienne Cain to guess what kind of car Ruby Killingsworth might drive if she ever chose to drive herself places, this one would have been her first guess.

It's a tiny, red, German two-seater with butter-soft black leather interior and the word MAVEN emblazoned on the license plate. If they'd wanted to be stealthy about their approach to the tower, this wasn't the way. But Ruby insisted, and Vivienne had been in no mood to argue—especially knowing it would have taken only a whiff of Ruby's magic to change her mind.

And she has to admit—riding in a convertible with the top down is almost as much fun as riding her motorcycle. Almost. She isn't entirely sold on what the wind is doing to her hair without the protection of a helmet.

Ruby, of course, has a silk scarf tied *just so* over her perfect coif. The fact that she'd paired it with red lipstick and oversized sunglasses, making her look like the living embodiment of old Hollywood sex appeal, is something Vivienne has to work hard not to let distract her.

She's not so much succeeding at that.

"Wow." Vivienne can't help the comment as the Ruby Tower comes into view. She looks at Ruby, who appears completely unsurprised as she turns the car to drive past the crowd on the sidewalk in front of the building. "That's a lot of people."

"What did you expect?" Ruby shakes her head. "I've had autographs hidden in that store from Dillon Dexter, Iden LaVorgna, MerMeg Gilal, and all five Young Dudes. If there wasn't a line around the block, someone in my PR department would be fired right about now."

45

Vivienne isn't sure whether she's impressed or terrified. She's known plenty of powerful people in her life, but never has she been in the presence of someone who wields so much power over so many people so casually. It's a disturbing, yet unquestionably alluring quality.

"All right, Ginger," Vivienne says, "I see you've gathered me a crowd. But this plan of yours has been a little light on the details up to this point. I'm presuming we're not about to go get in that line and wait our turn to get into the building."

"Of course not," Ruby scoffs.

"Mind telling me what we *are* going to do?"

"You know, for someone with so much hero experience, I would think you'd have a better grasp of what something like this entails." She shrugs as she takes a right-hand turn on the far side of the building.

"Hey, it's your plan, your building, and technically Ramisiel is *your* problem. So, could you let me know what you're thinking?"

Ruby looks around furtively, though Vivienne isn't sure why. There are no other cars on this stretch of road, nor, she guesses, should there be. It's a tiny spit of pavement between Ruby's building and Jaccob's that terminates in Starcom Plaza. With no parking on either side, and no access to either building, it's essentially a dead end. Vivienne has no idea why Ruby turned the car this way.

It's only a moment before she has an answer.

When Vivienne looks back at the Ruby Tower, its bricks are somehow moving. A section of wall seems to come apart and retract in several directions. Ruby steers the car off the road and onto the sidewalk, the yellow-painted curb flattening out just in time to give them a smooth ride.

"Not to worry, V," Ruby says as the car traverses the sidewalk and drives through the hole in the building left by the strangely moving bricks. "It's just the garage door."

Vivienne isn't sure she likes that Ruby noticed her discomfort, and neither is she remotely sure she dislikes the fact she's paying attention.

"You enchanted the garage door?" she asks, trying her best to sound cool, calm, and collected as Ruby pulls the car into a tiny space between the stretch Bentley they'd taken to Regency Heights and a Mercedes Benz town car with obvious bulletproofing.

"Not at all," Ruby answers. "That's a trick from Starcom Security. There's a thingamajig installed in my front bumper and some kind of receiver on the other side. Arsho can explain it if you really care to know."

She pulls off her sunglasses then unties the scarf from around her hair and allows it to fall onto the console between the car's two seats. Maybe the garage door is fancy billionaire tech, but the fact of Ruby's hair remaining perfectly styled despite the top-down drive *has to* be magic.

"No, that's——" Vivienne struggles not to lose her train of thought. "It's just I've never seen anything like it before."

Not strictly true, of course, but even The Raven doesn't make anything this smooth. His style is more ... brutalist.

"Everything Jaccob learned in building his building," Ruby says, flipping down her visor to examine herself in the little mirror on the underside, "he improved on for mine."

"But you two weren't together when——" Vivienne narrows her eyes in suspicion. She remembers the reason she came to Cobalt City in the first place. She once again wonders how much she doesn't know.

"Not yet." Ruby shrugs. "No."

"So wait," Vivienne begins, unsure of where she's going. Asking Ruby point blank if she meant to break up Jaccob's marriage isn't likely to get a straight answer. But, then again, Ruby has been surprisingly forthright about a lot of things. Maybe she's about to learn something. "Did you——?"

"Allow an attractive tech geek carte blanche to build everything his bearded little heart desires?" Ruby rolls her eyes as she flips the visor back up. "Why the hell would I do any different?"

"Right."

Once again, Vivienne isn't sure what to think. Liz was the one to leave Jaccob, not the other way around, but that dark little pit of suspicion at the back of her brain tells her there's more to Ruby's side of that story than anyone's said so far. She's intrigued. Maybe she'll include getting the whole damn story as part of her as-yet-determined fee for this demon extraction.

But first they'll have to extract the damn demon.

"We're taking my elevator up to the office." Ruby smooths the front of her floral silk blouse. "Security will walk you to the main business elevator bank and bring you down to the retail space through the back. That way, you'll already be inside when the doors open. People come in, they go crazy looking for autographs. Meanwhile, you look for this reprehensible bag of dicks that's apparently taken up residence in my building. I'm going to duck my head onto forty-six and curse Loki's name for a moment, just in case his tricky-ness decides to show up—either to help or to hinder."

"Is that—?" Vivienne only knows Loki peripherally. She isn't so much surprised at the thought the god might decide to spontaneously show up today as she is at the fact Ruby didn't think to mention it before now. "How likely is that, exactly?"

"You have no concept of *unpredictable* until you've met Loki." Ruby opens the door and steps out of the car.

"Yeah, okay, that makes sense." Vivienne fumbles to unfasten her seat belt.

Ruby isn't waiting; she just starts walking away. "And whether or not a certain immortal thorn in my side decides to come along for the festivities, I'll take the elevator from my second lobby down once I'm sure there's a crowd in the store."

"Damn," Vivienne says, unable to contain herself. "How many elevators have you got in this place?"

"Twelve," Ruby replies, as though that's a perfectly reasonable number.

"Twelve?"

"Two cars for retail, one of which also services the office. Four for the residential floors—that is, for residents and guests, one of them has a rear door to allow guests to exit through the store if they want to. Plus a freight elevator for resident use. Then there are two business elevators that go straight from the plaza side lobby to the company lobby, you came up one of those the other day. My private elevator, the one we're about to get in; my guest elevator, the one you joined me in when the mess hit the fan—currently out of order thanks to a certain extra-dimensional cretin. And finally, a freight elevator for business use—getting a grand piano up fifty stories takes some forethought."

"I guess." Vivienne doesn't know whether to be impressed or disgusted. She's never in her life seen such an obvious example of conspicuous consumption. Even Jaccob's ridiculous glass phallus only has six elevators. "So I'm taking one elevator up and another elevator down?"

"It's the fastest way."

"And you'll be taking another one?"

"Indeed," Ruby says. "Hopefully by the time I arrive you'll have found our unwanted guest."

"Just as likely he's waiting for you upstairs and follows you down." Vivienne shuts the car door behind her and hurries to catch up with Ruby, who's already a third of the way across the garage. For a moment, Vivienne considers asking whether she's going to lock the car, but then she remembers the outrageous moving-brick garage door and the fact this is quite possibly the most secure parking garage in the western world.

"Could you maybe not have reminded me I may have to share an elevator with that thing?" Ruby frowns as she presses the button beside a gleaming silver door: likely, the express elevator that will take them to the Goblin Records offices.

"Sorry," Vivienne says, catching up just as the door slides open. "I just want you to be prepared in case he's not where you expect."

"Thanks," Ruby says as she steps into the lift. "I think."

Vivienne follows Ruby into the elevator. It's smaller than she might have guessed, much smaller than the two she'd seen previously, but far more opulent than anything connected to a parking garage ought to be. All brass and mirrors. The thing doesn't even have buttons.

Probably there's some sort of fancy Starcom tech in here, same as the garage door. But with Ruby Killingsworth, everything feels like magic, and it's a little unsettling.

"If he isn't in the store when I get there, and he doesn't follow you immediately," Vivienne says as the door slides shut and the elevator starts moving, "I have a few tricks up my sleeve to lure him in."

"I want that to be reassuring," Ruby says.

"I meant it to be reassuring," Vivienne says, trying to sound cooler than she looks from all the angles she can't help but see in the elevator's inescapable reflective surfaces.

Ruby shakes off a shudder, and Vivienne resists the impulse to reach out to her. They're not there yet. Most likely never will be. And that's for the best. So instead, she pretends not to notice.

"You'll let me know when you have a read on him." Ruby unselfconsciously checks her makeup in the mirrored panel in front of her. "I'll tell you when I'm ready. Then you make him visible, everybody panics, you do what you do while I get the portal spun. You chase him into the portal, I shut the damn door behind him. You and I take advantage of the continued pandemonium to hop back on the elevator I rode down in, we change cars in the office, and we're up in the penthouse knocking back negronis before the retail staff can even get Arsho on their walkie."

"You mean before Stardust shows up?"

Vivienne isn't sure why she feels the need to needle Ruby when it comes to Jaccob. Maybe it's jealousy—until this redheaded vixen came along, she was the only woman who ever turned his head away from the paragon of feminine perfection he married, even if she didn't take advantage of it at the time. Or maybe it's just that Jaccob seems to be the one thing that consistently puts a tiny crack in Ruby's hard shell. Either way, she can't help herself.

"You know," Ruby replies, not bothering to meet Vivienne's eyes in any of their shared reflections, "I hadn't even thought about that. But I have to say the idea of denying him the opportunity to save the citizens pleases me."

"Doing a heroism before the hero can even show up?"

"Hmm." Her lip quirks into the faintest hint of a smile, one that would only be visible to a person who's paying close attention.

Vivienne is paying close attention.

"Would it help," Vivienne says, not fully believing she's about to poke an evil sorceress so hard right before they're supposed to be going into battle side-by-side, but somehow unable to resist the impulse, "if I told you I think he really loved you?"

Ruby snaps her head around faster than Vivienne has ever seen a mortal human move. "It would not." Something ripples through the air around her. "Also," she says before Vivienne has the chance to react, "love is a four-letter word, and I prefer it not be spoken in my presence."

Right then.

The doors open into Ruby's office. It's pristine, gleaming to a high-polished shine with no sign of the mayhem of two days prior. Vivienne steps off the elevator, wondering to herself how in the world she'd managed to miss the elevator door set into the office on her last visit. Knowing there had been an escape route less than ten steps away might have saved the both of them a measure of terror. But, then again, if it hadn't been for being so terrified, there was a real chance they'd never have leapt at each other the way they did. So perhaps it was for the best. Ruby steps out of the lift and brushes past Vivienne without another word.

A tall man in an oddly regal-looking security uniform approaches Vivienne from the doorway to the outer office. She wants to tell him to wait, so she can follow Ruby and have more of a conversation. But they're on a tight timeline. And Ruby doesn't want to talk.

The man gestures for her to come with him. So she does.

~

Ruby stands behind her desk and watches Vivienne leave. There's an odd feeling as soon as the door shuts, like some bit of energy had gone along with her. A burden, perhaps? Some stress she's been holding onto? Not anything Ruby wants to interrogate too closely—unless, of course, the thing that went with Vivienne had been the demon they were here to confront.

A quick divination suggests no demon lurking in wait—at least nowhere she can see immediately. Vivienne had shown her an easy divination for detecting demons—one that consumes less focus than the spell of revealing—and her magic isn't finding any trace of such a creature in her office, other than a faint smell like rotten eggs. Whether he'd followed Vivienne out or been elsewhere from the jump remains to be seen, but wherever Ramisiel is, he isn't *here*.

That's a relief, in exactly the way her office isn't.

Normally, this is a place of rest and reassurance for her—a place where she is always in complete control. It is from behind this desk that she issues orders and makes decisions that affect the flow of millions of dollars and just as many lives. Under her leadership, Goblin Records clears eleven figures a year, and not on the low end of that measure.

Now?

It doesn't feel remotely the same.

The office feels like it belongs to someone else, as though she's here for an interview, and she finds herself looking for pictures to pretend to be interested in.

Part of it is the state of the place. When she climbed out of the elevator, she expected it to be a wreck—a shredded, burned-out husk of itself—but if she hadn't personally witnessed a demon attack here, she would never believe anything out of the ordinary had happened. Any damage the demon did to her beautiful, reclaimed desk seems to have disappeared. Indeed, everything seems in perfect order, with neatly stacked papers, fresh flowers, and even her laptop, fully charged and plugged in, all in their proper places on her desk. All the pictures wait in their frames, smiling or looking fierce as expected ...

Wait.

Those aren't her pictures. Or, rather, they *are*, but she certainly never took any of them.

And it isn't that she doesn't remember; it's more like these pictures are impossible for her to have taken. Pictures of herself on a beach vacation in a lovely emerald-green one-piece, doing a karaoke duet, laughing at a joke at a business dinner at a high-class restaurant, kissing her dark-suited partner whilst wearing a suspiciously white and lacy dress, and one where she holds a dark-haired baby ... all of them with one other person. The same other person, whom she met just two days ago.

Vivienne Cain.

What the fuck? She doesn't even like babies—why is this giving her all these feelings?

She turns her attention back to her desk.

There's a digital frame she's sure wasn't there before today, scrolling through a slideshow of picnics and parties, holidays and home life—there are Christmas trees, Easter baskets, a Menorah—all of it tugging at heartstrings Ruby prefers not to acknowledge she so much as possesses. Vivienne. Jaccob. Little children. Candid shots of laughter and merriment. She hates it.

But somehow she can't look away.

Until she does.

And spots the tiny Comic Book Lady Vengeance rendered in plastic, standing beside the Stardust figure of similar vintage that she knows for a fact she keeps buried deep in a locked drawer. They sit in a prominent spot on her desk—in a place anyone on either side of it couldn't help but to see during a sit-down meeting.

A wave of something washes over Ruby, and she's experienced it so rarely it takes a second to identify the sensation: anxiety. It all feels so ... so wrong. And not just wrong, but wrong in a way that feels specifically designed to upset her. And if that be the case, it is definitely working.

"Demons like Ramisiel will do whatever they can to unsettle you—make you vulnerable," Vivienne had told her that morning. "Be ready."

Ruby thought she was. She knew full well how to steel herself for the kind of attack she was expecting. But she was *not* expecting this.

Her anxiety bleeds first into revulsion, and quickly into anger. Ramisiel is definitely due a firm chastising. After she thanks him for cleaning up her office, that is.

"One more time," Ruby says, and casts the divination Vivienne showed her. Again, no demon, though that unpleasant smell redoubles. She blows out a breath. Time to check on Loki.

She hopes Vivienne has the situation downstairs well in hand. She supposes she'll find out soon enough.

~

Standing on the mezzanine of the Goblin Records flagship store, Vivienne is aware of a faint chill running up and down her arms. It's been a while since she was in a place with this many music fans—or, as soon as the doors open—this many people at all.

The clock clicks over to 10 a.m., and the doors burst open to admit a flood of screaming young people. They appear from her vantage point as a tidal wave of loud colors and outlandish fashions, pouring into the red-carpeted galleria before the doors are even fully open. At first, it doesn't seem like they're aware of her, and she thinks for certain they'll crush her in a stampede of screeching teenage fans as they stream up the staircase in the kind of frenzy only young people seem to be capable of. And wouldn't *that* be an ironic fate for the once-great Lady Vengeance: trampled to death by a mob of kids.

But no, they notice her, and part around her like a jagged rock stabbed into the shore. They clamor toward the screens, the shelves, the posters, and keep shouting and murmuring and twitting, tweeping, twerking, or whatever it is. So, so much social media.

This doesn't seem so bad. For a second, she was worried.

Then she realizes it. Not a moment too soon, and probably too late to retreat without extreme consequence, she is suddenly, violently aware of the state of things around her.

This shouldn't be happening. The plan ... well, it wasn't flawless, but it shouldn't be going sideways basically instantly. She started this game already in check, if not checkmate. But how? Why?

And just like that, Vivienne has three spiraling revelations that leave her staggering.

Ramisiel knows.

He knows how her powers work.

He's known all along, and he's prepared for it. Far better than Ruby's halfway decent plan or Vivienne's half-cocked confidence.

But how?

In her mind, Vivienne feels a certain sense of mocking amusement, and a thought intrudes—one she knows definitely is not hers.

You think Azazel doesn't kiss and tell?

~

Ruby takes a breath and puts on her best game face.

The doors chime as they slide open.

"Loki?" she calls into the vestibule. She wants to sound glib, familiar, as though this is any other day, and she's come calling for any other purpose. But she's growing increasingly terrified.

Loki's space looks the way she'd imagined hers might have. The forty-sixth floor is wide open, with only load-bearing walls and columns to break up the areas. That was Loki's spec when they'd taken possession of this place. Ruby had spent countless hours and no small amount of money outfitting it to the god's exacting specifications. The acquisition of antiquities and sacred Norse objects had been an ordeal, but being host to the only space in the mortal realm into which a god could corporeally manifest without need of an avatar had paid her back in spades.

It had taken a substantial investment in both time and energy to curate this space, and she'd always enjoyed the time she spent here. Objects of power had always been a hobby of hers, and she did enjoy Loki's particular taste in opulent decor.

But this ... this isn't it.

The place is a shambles.

Statues, trinkets, and framed pictures lay strewn about. The furniture, some of it made from solid gold, has been, to a piece, upturned. The rugs are shredded, and the custom stitched down mattress reduced to nothing more than a generous dusting of feathers across nearly every flat surface in the vicinity of the mangled frame from whence it had been pulled.

She spots an icon of particular significance lying on the floor near the window behind Loki's upended throne: a carving of the trickster god themself. Not daring to use magic in a space this corrupted, Ruby hurries to retrieve it, examining its inlaid stones for damage before righting its usual pedestal and replacing the idol in its proper place.

"Loki," she calls again. She's trying to sound anything but frightened. Loki doesn't respond well to fear, and if they sense it, they're sure not to show. Ruby wonders if Vivienne can feel her terror from forty-five stories below; masking spells are useful and all, but she's sure this is the kind of dread that can be felt all the way on the other side of the Coil.

"Loki, darling," she addresses the empty room the way she always does when she hopes to garner their attention, "I know you said that demon isn't your problem, but you should see what he's done to the place. It's absolute bedlam in here. I've got a friend with me," she says, fingering the tattered velvet drapes. "We're going to kick its ass back to where it came from. You can join if you want." Ruby leans into the idol beside her and speaks into its crown as though it was a microphone. "You've got thirty seconds to show, or we're doing the deed without you."

Ruby feels magic in that moment. It isn't hers, but it doesn't feel like Loki, either—not exactly. A gust of wind blows past, a thing she knows to be impossible in this place, and yet she feels it as certainly as she does the pins in her hair.

Something hits her ankle, and she can't help but jump a little. She scoffs at her own skittishness when she looks down. There's nothing at her feet but a pile of feathers.

And a folded parchment, with Loki's gleaming red wax seal across it.

She has a feeling they won't be attending today's festivities.

Ruby bends down and snags the note. She pulls open the seal and unfolds the page, annoyed but unsurprised when it appears blank at first glance. This isn't an unusual state in which to find one of Loki's missives, and normally she wouldn't care in the slightest that their message required magic to reveal.

But normally she isn't standing in a demon-defiled shrine.

She supposes she can wait until later to read it. Either Loki is coming or they aren't, and the preponderance of evidence leans heavily toward *aren't*. Whatever this note says, it probably doesn't matter a hill of beans for the next couple of hours.

Ruby folds the note and slides it into her pocket as she turns to leave.

The moment she steps back toward the elevator, the wind kicks up again. It blows hard, alternating blistering hot and bitingly cold, growing ever stronger with every step she takes. Typical Loki: they've got something to say, but they don't quite have the balls to say it to her face. She knows she's not leaving without reading the note first.

"Fine!" she yells, shaking her head as she pulls the note from her pocket.

The wind ceases its onslaught immediately.

Ruby unfolds the parchment and frowns. The arcane energy in this place has already left a bad taste in her mouth. This is liable to leave her positively nauseated—not the feeling she'd hoped for heading into battle to banish a demon.

Ruby waves her fingers over the parchment, and runes burn themselves into existence on the skin. They'd just look like ancient art to a normal person, but the pact she's made with Loki gives her the power to understand. And this ...

"I made a deal," it says, and, worse, "you would have, too."

Involuntarily, Ruby lets slip a curse that is not acceptable in mixed company, even for gods. Worst of all, she's not alone.

It's behind her.

~

Fuck.

Also vomit.

Everywhere Lady Vengeance looks, roots have crept into ears, nostrils, and even eyes—the demon's tendrils interweave with hair and clothes, as though every single person in the room is but a marionette dancing on the creature's strings. And when they look at her, there is no terror in their gazes—only rage.

"Great."

Lady Vengeance raises her claw to ward off a set of grasping hands. The rabid fan who possesses said hands doesn't flinch, even as the talons stab through their palm like something out of a horror movie, and it's Lady Vengeance who has to pull back, lest she leave the hapless thrall maimed. She came here ready to fight a tree demon, one she wouldn't worry about hurting, but a bunch of kids whose only crime is being in the right place at the wrong time? Well, that and some of those haircuts are just *utterly* inexcusable. Not the undercuts, though—Lady Vengeance makes a mental note to try that out, presuming she gets out of this mess alive.

It seems like the sort of thing Ruby would love, or it would make her thoroughly irritated, and either way, it would be worth it. Ruby's fingers stroking the side of her mostly shaved head, the little hairs prickling them both ...

Shit, why is she thinking about Ruby's taste in haircuts at a time like this? She has to pay attention if she's going to ...

One unusually large fan, at least twice Lady Vengeance's size, slams into her, knocking her stumbling back in a shattering stagger through a case of numerous awards and prize records. It's safety glass, but she still feels dozens of bright slits of pain cut open on her legs and unarmored hand and arm. They're instantly on her again, and she has to take a totally defensive stance, protecting her head and neck. The demon thralls have no particular skill, but they do have enthusiasm and bulk, and that's enough in close quarters.

"Sorry, Ginger," she says through gritted teeth as she holds off pummeling fists with raised arms, "but you did say this is why you have insurance."

She draws on the reserves of fear energy and sculpts it into a growing ball of force between her hands. Tendrils lash out and push at the seemingly endless wave of thralls, but they weaken as she spends more and more energy. More thralls are coming, and she isn't sure she has enough power in reserve to push them back and carve an escape route ...

"*Vengeance*," Azazel says in her mind. "*Call upon me—*"

Does she really have a choice?

"No," she says, teeth grinding painfully. "I'll die first."

"*Then I'll see you in hell.*"

Her eyes flare with purple energy. No. *No.*

"No!" she screams.

Lady Vengeance opens herself to Azazel's power, her choice in the matter overwhelmed by the demon's frenzied urge to take control. Her anger flashes, and then is gone, drowned by the satisfaction of Azazel's consciousness as he forces his thoughts into her head. Shapes her power in ways she could never manage herself.

The thralls pressing in around her abruptly fly back, flung away as if by a great wind. In their midst stands Lady Vengeance, hair swirling around her, eyes blazing with darkness. With grim purpose, she flings out her right hand, purple lightning dancing between the tines of her claw, and sends a wave of rippling force forth to shatter a hole clear through the window, taking much of the surrounding wall with it. The thralls pull themselves up, slavering and seething, but Lady Vengeance hardly notices. She's staring down at her hands, around which purple fire continues to lick and course.

"*You will never not be mine.*"

Abruptly, she runs for the opening, as hands claw at her from every side, and hurls herself into the Cobalt City sky.

~

The gnarled roots that are the demon's fingers—and hopefully only that—begin to snake along Ruby's shoulders, winding toward her ears, her nose, her mouth, as though to turn her into a puppet like those poor hapless fools she'd tried to use as bait for her trap.

She realizes, only too late, the trap was for her.

Then the windows of Loki's sanctum shatter open and something—*someone*—comes flying through.

At first, for one thoroughly embarrassing moment, she thinks—even wishes—it's Stardust, Cobalt City's most famous hero. He would whisk her up in his arms, all would be forgiven, and then he'd jet away to her private house in the Caribbean (who cares about things like how long that flight would take?), where he would announce he has left Liz for good this time, and they would make love using all the tricks she taught him and a few that surprise even her, and in the morning he would make pancakes and mimosas, and she would tastefully turn down the carb bomb but graciously accept the sparkly drink, and then they would live happily ever after, or at least until she got bored.

But it's *not* Jaccob Stevens, and a good thing too, because if she's scared enough to imagine a whole hetero-monogamous happy ending with *him* of all people, she's in dire straits.

No, instead she feels her terror draining away, replaced with a kind of cool detachment. It should be impossible for anyone to manipulate her emotions through her magic, but some sorcerers grow very powerful when angry, and Lady Vengeance is *pissed*.

The lapsed goth girl supervillain crashes through the wall-size windows, blazing with purple energy in the form of a full suit of laminate armor such as a samurai might wear, a single wing of purple fire flaring from her shoulder. The wing doesn't seem to be flapping—her flight has nothing to do with the energy manifestation, but is just her will alone. Then she smashes her fist into the demon so hard it flies back against the opposite wall. And through it.

Ruby is about to say something—drop some witticism, maybe—but Lady Vengeance looks at her with those burning purple eyes, and her mouth goes entirely dry, her body goes rigid with excitement, and the rest of her ... *well*.

Lady Vengeance wraps her arms around Ruby and pulls her in close, which really doesn't help with the trying to speak thing. "Hang on," Lady Vengeance says, her voice deeper and darker than usual.

Ruby manages not to say the first two things that rise to her lips: "sure," which would sound too vulnerable, or "always," which would absolutely *not* do. Instead, she just nods slightly.

And just like that, Lady Vengeance flies them out the destroyed window.

~

About fifteen minutes later, they sit in a bar a few blocks away from Starcom Plaza, close enough that they can see the smoke rising from Ruby's building and hear the sirens of the still arriving emergency vehicles, but far enough away Jaccob Stevens won't swoop in and do what he does best: save the day.

Vivienne's pretty sure neither of them could deal with that. Not today.

Ruby takes a sip of her very dirty martini. Between the casual and composed way she holds it and the five minutes she spent fixing up her makeup in the bathroom, Ruby seems entirely at ease, as though she hadn't just fought a demon.

For her part, Vivienne is shaking too much to be jealous.

"All right, well, that wasn't bad, for our first try," Ruby says, with the air of someone considering a desperate boy band's first test recording. "I think we both learned some valuable information that will make our next foray—"

"Next? No, no, no," Vivienne says, smacking her hands on the table. "This is it, Ginger. I spend twenty-four hours with you, and I open myself back up to the demon lord who possessed me as a kid and—"

"Wait, what?" Ruby asks. "You did *what?*"

Vivienne clams up and stares at her, serious as the grave. "Look," she says at length. "It's over, ok? Thanks for the food, the drinks, and the sex was pretty fantastic, but that's it. We're done. Enough fucking with my life." She stands abruptly, leaving her double bourbon untouched. "I never want to see you again, got it?"

Ruby glances first at the abandoned drink, then stares at Vivienne levelly, her expression completely unreadable and her emotions entirely concealed under her magic. "Got it."

"Good." Vivienne turns to storm away, then pauses, patting at her empty pocket. "My fucking phone."

Ruby is already tapping something on her very small, very high-tech smartphone.

"What are you doing?" Vivienne asks.

"Calling you a car," she says. "And arranging for my plane to take you back to Seattle."

"I don't need your fucking charity."

"Perhaps not, but you *do* need a ride. And it's honestly the least I can do. That is, until you get back to me with your pay rate."

"Right," Vivienne says. In the chaos of the last several hours, she'd almost forgotten the matter of her compensation. "Ten days, right? That was the deal."

"Correct." Ruby extends her hand with Vivienne's phone perched atop her palm.

Vivienne makes a point not to touch Ruby's fingers as she takes it back, but she can't help but marvel at the fact Ruby's manicure has remained intact.

"And I did say travel included," Ruby adds, curling her lip into a smile that somehow says she still means business whilst also being as smug as Vivienne imagines a person can possibly get.

"You did. In addition to my fee." Vivienne wasn't about to let this ginger villain's preferred mode of transport put a limit on her eventual demands.

"Indeed."

"Your plane?"

"One of them."

Vivienne opens her mouth to snap back at her, then closes it. "Will there be booze on board?"

"Darling ... have we met?"

"Top shelf?"

"Always."

"Fan-fucking-tastic."

ROUND FOUR: SOCIAL DRINKING

Vivienne isn't sure at first that she's actually awake. Her dreams have been known to be every bit as fucked up as the situation she finds herself in at the moment. But the ripple of magic and the smell of expensive perfume are enough to tell her this is real: Ruby Killingsworth really is standing at the foot of her bed in her disheveled Seattle apartment. There's no way this will end well.

"What are you doing here?" she manages to groan. "Wait ... no ... I mean ... how do you know where I live?" Vivienne forces herself upright to look her unexpected guest in the eye.

In her impeccable purple dress, Ruby crosses her arms and quirks her eyebrow. Fair enough: she doesn't seem like the type of woman to dignify such a question with a response.

"Right. You're an evil mastermind." Vivienne looks at the clock: 3:45 p.m. Way too early for a Saturday. She flops back down onto her side and gathers the pillow into a bunch beneath her head. "So, back to my first question. What are you doing here?"

"I came for you," Ruby replies flatly.

"Several times, if I recall correctly." Vivienne sits up. "But this is an awful long way for you to have traveled for a repeat performance."

It's more than that, of course. They spent quite the weekend in Cobalt City after their less-than-successful demon battle. Vivienne's intention to storm out immediately had been fouled by Ruby's presence in her master bedroom when she'd insisted on getting her bag herself instead of asking a butler to bring it down. "I never want to see you again," had turned into "one for the road" had turned into "what the hell" over and over again until finally a car had shown up on Monday morning to take Vivienne to the airport. They hadn't done much talking that weekend, nor had they so much as said goodbye to each other in the morning. Honestly, Vivienne liked it that way. She'd thought that was the end of it. Truly. Forever.

She really should have known to expect this development.

"While that's not at all what I meant—" Ruby steps forward to lean over the wrought iron foot of the bed, putting their faces close together. "I do think we can add that to the schedule of activities."

"Good." Vivienne leans forward to kiss her, but Ruby withdraws slightly, just out of easy reach. She smiles with those pouting, heart-shaped lips of hers.

"After."

"Fine." This was beginning to be a pattern. Not that Vivienne minded. Some supernatural excitement followed by a spate of mind-bending orgasms wasn't a bad way to spend a weekend. But she remembers Azazel's touch, and it makes her whole soul shudder.

Ruby still looks sly and smug. "I like how you didn't ask 'after what?'."

"And I like that you wear stockings and a garter belt as a matter of course. So." Vivienne inches down the bed until she can place her hands on top of Ruby's. "What's the problem?"

"That demon in my tower."

"Ramisiel? Let me guess—"

"He's still there."

"Ginger," Vivienne says. "It's been a month, and you still haven't got rid of that fucker?"

Ruby looks a bit annoyed. "I ... could use a consult."

"What, the mighty sorceress can't take care of some pesky demon with her magic? I mean, if I could punch him through a wall, surely you could do better?"

"I'm afraid it's a bit more complicated." Ruby leans in again.

Vivienne could pounce if she really wanted to, but she doesn't, instead letting the tension build as their lips hover mere inches apart.

Dammit, Ruby needs her help. Vivienne knows in her bones that she can't defeat Ramisiel without channeling Azazel, and she isn't about to do that again. But ... *fuck*.

"I guess I can do complicated," Vivienne whispers.

"Mmm. I remember." Ruby touches Vivienne's face, her fingers tingling with their own electricity that has only a little to do with

64

magic. Ruby flushes a little and looks away. "But you should probably get dressed."

"Way to spoil the mood, Ginger." Vivienne slides out of bed, rubbing her aching head. Her Belltown apartment is even more of a mess than usual—hardly suitable for normal guests, let alone a mega-wealthy evil mastermind, but Ruby's being exceptionally polite and patient, averting her eyes from all the clutter.

Vivienne reaches for the half-empty bottle of Jack Daniels on the dresser, but Ruby takes it before she can. "Sorry, darling," she says, clapping her hand twice over the bottle's mouth. "We're going to do this bit sober."

"Wonderful."

Ruby meets her gaze for a moment, then looks away. She takes a swig of the bottle, scowls, and wipes her mouth. She's nervous, Vivienne realizes.

"So tell me about 'complicated'," Vivienne says, "and what I can do to help. As long as it isn't 'let's go back to the tower, V,' because that isn't happening. I'm not going back there."

"Not the plan. I respect boundaries, remember?"

"I do." Vivienne waves her to continue.

"You're the one who said you wanted a proper introduction to Loki."

"I did say that, didn't I?" Vivienne still isn't sure what possessed her to name that as her payment, but she had. And now, apparently, it was about to happen.

"Indeed." Ruby grins as she swirls the brown liquor in the bottom of the bottle. "I can't imagine why you'd want to meet him, other than for the obvious."

"Him, eh? That's not what I heard."

"Him, her, them, and a few others. Loki inhabits *all* pronouns." Ruby chews her lip. "I'm a little curious as to how you knew I knew him well enough to make that happen."

"Surprised?" Vivienne asks. She reaches toward her open dresser drawer and grabs a black t-shirt that says Nasty Woman on the front. She drank enough the previous night that the emotions she's picking up are a dull blur, and of course she picks up nothing from Ruby. The woman may have flown across the country and swooped in for an afternoon booty call, but she doesn't trust Vivienne enough to drop her protective mantle. Smart.

"A little," Ruby says back before taking a dainty sip of Vivienne's whisky.

"I'd like to tell you some bullshit story about arcane research and tapping into supernatural energies. I know you're into that kind of stuff." Vivienne pulls the shirt on over her head and looks around for her jeans. "But the truth is: before I ever came to see you, I called Jaccob and asked about your deal. He may have angrily grumbled something about suspecting you were chummy with Loki, which tracks with something I felt in your tower, and something you said before we tried to banish Ramisiel the last time. The forty-sixth floor is a temple, isn't it?"

"Hrm." Ruby sounds mildly irritated. "And how is our ex?"

"Insufferable," Vivienne says. "Liz is doing well, too, if you were wondering."

"I wasn't." Ruby arranges her hair, which absolutely doesn't need the attention. "But yes, I let Loki have the forty-sixth floor in exchange for some help with a problem last year. It's all set up so he can come and go as he pleases. It's the only place in this whole slice of the Coil Loki can corporeally manifest without using an avatar—an access point he's come to enjoy greatly, if you get my drift. But apparently he can't be bothered to shut the damned door behind him."

Vivienne sucks in a breath. That was a revelation she thought she'd been ready for, but wasn't. Apparently suspecting Ruby had dealings with Loki and knowing for sure they'd been lovers were two very different states of being. But that would be a conversation for later. There are more pressing matters at present.

"So the demon can just ... slither back in? Whenever he wants?"

"Exactly. But Loki's selfish ass maintains it's not his problem."

"That sounds about right. So you don't want more help fighting the demon. You want me to help you persuade Loki to keep it from coming and going. And you came all this way to ask in person. You must really need my help," Vivienne says as she stands there, picking through the tangles in her own hair. "Or else you really like me."

"Why not both?" Ruby asks. Her grin is positively wicked.

"Both is good."

Ruby coughs, pointedly and adorably. "Clothes?"

"Right." Vivienne spots her jeans in a wad on the floor. She toes her way into the right leg before bending to pull them on—

one leg and then the other. It's hard to do without stumbling, especially with her still-building hangover.

"There is one other thing," Ruby confesses, a knowing expression crossing her features that makes Vivienne feel something between turned on and terrified.

"Do I even want to know?" Vivienne asks. She hops up to shrug her jeans up and over her hips.

"He's here in Seattle."

"What?" Vivienne's not sure she's following. "Loki has an avatar in Seattle, or—?"

"No. No. Loki himself is here in Seattle."

"But I thought you said he—they—can only manifest without an avatar in your building?"

"Oh, you heard that right." Ruby rolls her eyes as she takes another swig from Vivienne's bottle of Jack.

There's something irresistibly attractive about someone so well-heeled and refined knocking back belts of cheap whiskey straight from the bottle like a redneck at a bonfire. Vivienne is sorely tempted to ignore the purpose of Ruby's visit and jump her bones here and now. But there are things she needs to understand first. And, besides, she's already gotten dressed.

"I'm not sure I'm following," Vivienne says. "If they can't manifest here, then how—?"

"No one bends the rules quite like Loki. He has this thing he likes to do: spin a nice, neat, all-but seamless portal between his place and some mortal hangout. Loki can't pass through it, but the unsuspecting mortals can come and go as they please. And by 'as they please' I do mean 'at Loki's bidding'. It's mostly for sex, sometimes for politics, and never for very long at a stretch."

"So Loki's opened one of those here, right?"

Ruby nods. "I thought you and I would pay his tricksterness a call."

Vivienne didn't know all of that, and it unsettles her a bit to think of trickster gods just popping in to fuck and fuck with whoever they want. She smiles it off, though.

"So ... you're not just here for sexytimes?"

"First things first." Ruby keeps her face pointedly blank. "A little business, we get a right darling trickster god to hear us out, followed by a roll in the hay?"

67

A roll in the hay. Who even calls it that? Ruby's so delightfully retro.

"Sounds like fun." Vivienne quirks an eyebrow. "Should I bring my motorcycle?"

Ruby tosses her head back and cackles. "Yes," she says firmly, "yes, you should."

~

As the motorcycle zooms up Denny toward Capitol Hill, her petite frame pressed to Vivienne's strong back, arms around her for support, Ruby has to admit she's been looking forward to this. And not just because she's been waiting for a chance to wear the vintage '50s bomber jacket she bought to go with the dress she picked for this occasion.

When her powers had first begun to manifest in middle school, Ruby had immediately used them to go from awkward kid to it-girl, lounging in the plush passenger seat of one high school boy's souped-up muscle car or another in the parking lot of the shopping mall or roller rink. By the time she was due for a proper teenage rebellion, she was already hip deep in the music business. Money had always meant more than enjoyment, a fact she'd parlayed into a worldwide media empire. Still, she'd sometimes wondered what it might be like to be a rebel, cruising with some greasy punk or a stoner on a grumbling bike, red hair streaming out from under a helmet. That had always seemed beneath her—indecent and probably extremely uncomfortable.

This, though—it's like taking part in a fantasy she never knew she had, weaving in and out of traffic, leaving a streak of purple light in their wake. Horns honk, and they come close to causing at least one accident, but Vivienne doesn't seem to care. Ruby never draws attention to herself like this, but she eases into it quickly, her uncertainty turning quite rapidly into exhilaration. The motor thrums, the power ripples between her legs, and Ruby understands for the first time why someone might ride one of these loud, clanking things.

That, and Vivienne's jacket, which smells pleasingly of old leather and scotch. Ruby burrows in tight and presses her face into the woman's shoulder.

It doesn't hurt that it's a beautiful Seattle evening, either. They grabbed an afternoon snack for her, breakfast for Vivienne, from a taco truck, and Ruby was glad she made herself eat the plebeian food, which was unexpectedly and utterly delicious. Vivienne watched her, bemused and on the verge of a snicker, and Ruby felt comfortable for the first time since sealing her haunted tower with powerful forbiddance magic. The sun started to set early, so by rush hour, they're driving away from a really epic sunset.

Vivienne coasts to a stop half a block up from their destination and wedges the kickstand down. "You can let go now, Princess. We're safe."

"Hmm." Ruby releases her grudgingly. She was holding very tight, but not out of fear. "What happened to Ginger? I liked Ginger."

"Did you?" Vivienne helps her down from the bike, and Ruby lets her. "Well, whatever you want, Your Worship."

"I know what you're doing."

"Is it working?"

"Obviously." She looks around, drawing in her coat against the cold. "Did you have to park so far away?"

Vivienne points to the urban spa and massage parlor they're standing in front of. "I figured you'd want to powder your nose. Make an entrance. I don't know how much you know about the place you said we're going, but I can assure you it's more my usual speed than it is yours. I'm guessing you'll want to get the appropriate variety of dolled up."

"Oh." Ruby's face lights with a genuine grin. "Hell yes."

"I can wait here," Vivienne says, "or go grab us a coffee—"

But Ruby snatches up her hand. "Oh no. No no no. You're going to tell me more about this place so I'm sure to do this right. And at the very least, you're getting your face done."

"What's wrong with my face?"

"*Darling.*"

~

Vivienne hasn't been to a spa in years, but she always remembered the experience as lasting all day. Ruby, on the other hand, is a pampering professional, and they are in and out of there, plucked, exfoliated, groomed, trimmed, and made-up like models in under three hours, with time to spare for a massage Vivienne has to confess she really needed. Apparently, given enough money to throw around, almost anything is possible.

Once fully informed about the nature of the place Loki has chosen to spin up their Seattle honey-hole, Ruby also dispatches minions to fashion boutiques on Capitol Hill, and they return throughout the treatment with big bundles of clothes, bought sight-unseen. At first, Vivienne assumes the clothes are all for Ruby, like somehow she needed to do away with the sequined purple number she showed up in, but as it turns out ...

"For me?" Vivienne frowns as the attendants work on her lower back. "Oof, right there." She moans. "What's wrong with my clothes? I've been to this place before, you know, dressed just like this. I don't really think the wardrobe change is necessary."

"*Darling.*"

One private fitting room slash make-out session later, and Vivienne finds herself in quite a nice little black dress that gives her flashbacks to her time in the Agents of Awesome, when she was a hot little eighteen-year-old who didn't know better. This get-up would definitely make Wren blush furiously and Dirk start drooling flames. She waits in the lobby while Ruby finishes her own outfit change. Apparently, the purple dress wasn't sufficient for whatever Vivienne's primer on tonight's destination had brought to mind. It seems unnecessary until she arrives, and Vivienne's eyes widen a little.

"Wow."

Ruby smiles. "Let's go."

~

It's almost midnight when they blow through the doors of the club on Broadway in what seems like slow motion—just as a particularly bold song comes on the speakers, filling the darkened room with a robust beat and the vocals of a pair of singers who just don't give a fuck.

Vivienne looks great in her black dress with the plunging neckline, because of course she does. Ruby's always had an eye for fashion, and the spa treatment shaved at least ten years off Vivienne's face. She does fill the dress out quite well, and her natural coloration lends itself to the dark tones of both dress and

70

make-up. The collar is the best touch, though, with the three feet or so of silver chain; a delicate, refined bit of fetish-wear that didn't make Vivienne blink an eye.

The attention of the club is mostly on Ruby, though, and not just because she's holding the other end of said chain. She's all in elegant silver, her blood-red hair done up in floating clouds, and wears heels that give her a slight height advantage, even with Vivienne's thigh-high boots. She knows it's a good color for her, and the intrigued glances of the patrons confirm that. If anything's going to catch Loki's eye, it'll be this.

Their venue-appropriate, attention-grabbing wardrobe is entirely the point. They stroll in, pause for a second to see and be seen, then Ruby jerks the chain and brings Vivienne into her embrace.

"Ow," Vivienne says, feigning discomfort.

Ruby's sparkling purple lips curl, and she runs one hand down Vivienne's arm. "Get us drinks, will you, pet?"

"Laying it on a little thick, eh?" Vivienne asks.

"Drama. I can be gentler if you like."

"I wasn't complaining."

Let off the lead for the moment, Vivienne heads for the bar, where several patrons make way for her as a matter of course. She utterly ignores the guy who attempts small-talk and silences the one who tries to hit on her with a single withering glare. It's really quite lovely.

Meanwhile, that frees up Ruby to scan the club for their mark. The place is packed with people watching fancifully dressed dancers of various gender presentations work their stuff on poles, in cages, and, most significantly, on a stage in a side room that's appointed like a miniature theater. It's a performance she doesn't recognize, though she suspects she could guess "tribute to Chicago" and have a fifty-fifty chance of calling it correctly.

And there, in that chamber, in the middle of a sinuous huddle of attractive young flesh, is the entity of the hour. Loki presents as they typically do in a liberal bastion like Seattle, in a gender-agnostic way that defies easy classification, specifically geared to be as attractive as possible to as many people as possible. And it's definitely working, as Ruby counts at least six lovers attached to the God of Mischief before she has to give up because it becomes tough to tell people apart. It's only then she's able to detect the portal, the rippling of arcane energy barely visible amid the maelstrom of energies in the club.

But it's there, it's solidly spun, and when she works to breathe it in, it's as familiar as her own welcome mat. This is Loki's magic. She's found it, and she's found him.

This is going to be a fucking *treat.*

With a breath, she heads over to the entrance to the side theater, but a big tattooed mook gets in her way. He frowns down at her from a full foot and a half. The height differential gives him an excellent view of her not inconsiderable cleavage, but he doesn't seem remotely interested.

"Hello," Ruby says. "You're in my way."

"Private party," the bouncer says in a vaguely northern European accent. "You innt on the list."

"You haven't checked any list."

"No need. Innt no list, and even if there is, you innt on it."

"Hrm."

Ruby pours a bit of the old charm magic into their interaction, but it dissolves to no effect, and the bouncer doesn't so much as budge. A tiny revealing spell later, and she knows the reason: the bouncer's visage turns translucent, with another creature interposed over him. Something much larger, brawnier, and uglier.

A troll—of course.

It makes sense that Loki would bring supernatural backup, rather than trust his security to mundane humans, who could be notoriously unreliable. Case in point, Vivienne at the bar, who is flirting quite obviously with the tattooed bartender. Not that Ruby blames her—she's starting to understand the youths' interest in undercuts—but they're on a mission, dammit.

Change of plans.

The point here is to take Loki by surprise. Loki likes that, and he likes Ruby. But he's been avoiding her since the day the tower got busted up. Maybe if she found a way to tell Loki she was here, he'd beckon her to his side and brag to his assembled entourage what a powerful mortal had come such a considerable distance just for the joy of his company. Under normal circumstances, that's absolutely what he would do.

But these are not normal circumstances. Tonight, Loki would be just as likely to shut down the portal and run, trapping no telling how many hapless mortals on the other side. Ruby doesn't so much give a damn about the fate of Loki's congregants, but it took her no small amount of effort to track her immortal acquaintance to this place, and she does not want to see all that work wasted.

They're going to have to go about this differently.

Ruby arrives at the bar just as the bartender finishes pouring the third and fourth shots of whiskey, leaning on her hand and smiling at something Vivienne said. She sets down the bottle and starts idly toying with the slack silver chain between her fingers. Vivienne's apparently already had two shots, and beside them rises a daiquiri with a cherry, apparently for Ruby. She seizes the elegant glass and puts it to her lips. Strong and very good.

"There you are." Vivienne smiles at her. "I was just telling Chrissy here—"

Ruby raises one finger to cut her off until she finishes the daiquiri. "Go serve someone else," Ruby says with an edge of compulsion, and Chrissy gets a dazed look and wanders away.

"Hey," Vivienne says. "Possessive, much? That's kind of a turn-off."

Idly, Vivienne reaches for one of the shots, but Ruby grabs it before she can touch it and knocks it back, then the other. The alcohol burns, and she shakes her head. That's a lot of booze she just drank, but she's focused.

"You know what," Vivienne says, impressed. "Never mind. Right back in."

"Come on." Ruby takes the silver chain and hauls Vivienne toward the back door of the club.

"Where are we going?" Vivienne asks as the door comes open with a flick of her companion's wrist. Sometimes Ruby's magic is terrifying, but other times it's unbelievably hot.

There isn't time for Ruby to speak before the answer becomes apparent. Vivienne eyes the ink black stretch limo parked in the alley. It's shiny, and long, but nondescript as limousines go. It's nowhere near as posh as the Bentley Ruby had picked her up in back in Cobalt City. Possibly a service hire—likely the headquarters for a bar-hopping bachelorette soiree or milestone birthday debauchery.

A tall man in a cheap suit stands beside the car's door. Ruby is headed straight for him.

"That's ... not our limo," Vivienne says.

"Of course it isn't," Ruby replies as the driver moves to open the door.

Vivienne has no idea what exactly is going on, but she's not in the mood to argue.

Ruby stops short, puts her hand on the small of Vivienne's back, and guides her through the door into the car.

"Then what—?" Vivienne is confused, but somehow not displeased as Ruby slides onto the leather seat beside her.

The driver shuts the door behind them. The car is otherwise empty. The ceiling lights dance in a flicker of blues and greens— dim enough to keep outside eyes from peeking, but bright enough to see by. Good. Ruby reaches around to start trying to unfasten the silver dress.

"So—" Vivienne puts her hands on Ruby's hips and speaks in a slightly slurred voice. "It's not my first time in the back of a car, but—"

"Not right now," Ruby says. "Help me out of this dress."

"You know I was kidding, right?"

Ruby gives her a sharp look. "If you're not going to help, at least take your clothes off."

Vivienne frowns. "We're getting undressed but we're not fooling around?"

"Correct."

"Mind telling me what the hell we *are* doing, then?"

"Loki has a troll guarding him. Trolls only respect strength. So you've got to take point, since you're obviously stronger and scarier than me."

"Ok—" Vivienne unzips and lets the dress fall around her. "So why are we getting naked?"

"We have to switch the power dynamic. It's—you know what, it's complicated. Just don't worry about it. I should mess up my lipstick, too."

"Also because of the troll?"

"Hmm." Ruby slides closer and kisses the hollow between Vivienne's jaw and her ear. "Let's go with yes."

Vivienne smiles. "Ah."

~

They make their way back through the crowded nightclub; if they caught some eyes before, now it's even more so. And why not? Their hair is mussed, their lipstick smeared almost to the point of nonexistence, and they're wearing each other's outfits.

The silver getup fits Vivienne pretty well, and she feels like some sort of actress in a high-budget movie. She's a little thinner than Ruby, so she was concerned the black wouldn't fit her right, but she needn't have worried. If anything, it looks better on Ruby than it ever did on her, and Vivienne suspects a lot of clothes are like that. Even the collar and chain.

The troll bouncer's eyes widen slightly when they approach, then he steps aside without a word.

Ruby Killingsworth is a dangerous, dangerous woman.

Why does she need Vivienne tonight, again? Ruby hasn't been super clear on that. It's been a fun night out, and it's not like Vivienne takes many of those, but she really hopes Ruby doesn't need her to fuck somebody up. Unless that's the kind of thing Ruby considers foreplay.

Loki waits at the end of the hall, at the center of a mass of very attractive people of various skin tones, hair colors, and gender presentations. Vivienne has crossed paths with the God of Mischief on one or two occasions, but they were always more of a threat for Supergroup overall to deal with, not Lady Vengeance personally. Loki seemed to have a thing about her sister Athena, actually, which would make sense, considering the whole mythology connection. And they were never really a villain so much as a meddler—a schemer—someone who continually complicated things but always seemed to weasel out of a righteous pummeling.

Athena probably tried to keep her kid sister away from Loki because she'd have liked them too much. She certainly does now.

Loki is, for lack of a better term, gorgeous. Their features are androgynous and striking, their partly bared body vibrating with barely contained power. Looking at them, Vivienne thinks the whole club is moving in slow motion, with Loki sitting at the center, like the eye of a storm. Their emerald gaze captures her, and despite hers and Ruby's bad-ass roll, she has to admit Loki's attention gives her pause.

That, and the ambient lust and pleasure, which she soaks up like spilled rosé. It's sweet and light and it makes her a little tipsy just being in the building. She was picking up some pretty strong desire from the bartender—Vivienne has a demonstrable weakness for redheads, particularly with undercuts—but now, in close proximity to the actual God of Mischief ... *woof.* It's like they're sex personified, and she's not too proud to admit it makes her weak in the knees.

Not so Ruby, however. She marches right up to Loki, heedless of the chain in Vivienne's hand, and hooks one elegant heel around the neck of one of the God of Mischief's kneeling lovers, moving said individual aside.

Vivienne is hoping for a convenient reveal, but all she catches is a flash of really excellent abs and a mostly unbuttoned pair of skin-tight emerald-green hot pants.

"My favorite mortal," Loki says. "What a surprise. I didn't expect to see you on this side of the country, much less on this side of one of my—what do you call them—'fuck portals'?"

Ruby frees her foot with a deft twist of her ankle, then steps right on the chair between Loki's legs. The aggressive move prompts a stir among Loki's attendants, but Ruby doesn't seem to care. She leans forward, looming over the indolent god. "Howdy there, neighbor. You never call, you never write—"

Loki sets aside a martini and looks up, bemused. "This doesn't seem like a bit much? The whole angel and devil thing?"

"Nothing's too much for me, darling," Ruby says. Then, to emphasize, she puts a hand on the inside of Loki's thigh. "Nothing."

"Interesting." Loki's eyes flick to Vivienne. "And what's this? Your captive angel, eh?"

"That's Lady Vengeance," Ruby says. "You know, one of those hero types, only not?"

"Truly." Loki's eyes narrow and their voice drops into a purr. "I didn't recognize you, Ms. Cain, without all the black leather and the purple eyeshadow."

"You're a lot less masc than you were last time I saw you," Vivienne says. "It suits you."

Ruby looks from one of them to the other. "You know each other? I thought the point of this was a proper introduction."

"We've crossed paths," Vivienne says. "Naughty godling here was trying to conquer the world, of course."

"Tsch. The human world is boring." Loki leans to one side and kisses a pale-skinned woman in the hollow behind her ear, making her shiver all over. "Your comics, on the other hand. I particularly enjoyed your *Dark Vengeance* run. Compelling. Profound. Erotic. Like a dark, old wine, sipped during a warm bath."

"That's a really poetic way to describe softcore porn in comic book form."

"I drank of the poet's mead." Loki puts their little finger to their lips. "Don't tell anyone."

Vivienne smirks. "Next you're going to offer me a glowing review of *Dial V for Vengeance*."

"Well, now that you mention it—"

"What is happening right now?" Ruby asks, her mouth twisting dangerously close to a pout.

"Oh, nothing," Vivienne says. "The God of Mischief here appears to be a fan."

"God," Ruby says, her voice dripping with sarcasm.

"Yes?" Loki smiles at them. "Thank you for the formal introduction to your friend, there, but I'm not sure what you're looking for tonight, Goblin Queen." The god gestures at Ruby's exquisite heel, still grinding into the chair between their legs. "Now if you don't mind—?"

Ruby removes the indicated foot, freeing up Loki's nether area for easy access, and the god goes back to attending their many, many celebrants.

Goblin Queen? Vivienne mouths, but Ruby gives her a sharp look. Vivienne looks away from exactly what the big, perfectly cut gentleman with the bowtie is doing to Loki's lower parts, and instead checks out the stage. She's been known to enjoy some burlesque in her day—even danced a few shows when she was younger, not particularly well—and the performers tonight seem quite skilled and equally enthusiastic. Also, so many feathers.

"Lord Liesmith—darling." Ruby forces her mouth to smile. "I'm here because I need a favor."

"I see." Loki takes a break from slipping their long, dexterous tongue into interesting places and goes to kissing instead. "And I owe you this favor because—?"

"Because it involves the tower in which we both live," Ruby says. "My tower. In which you live. Rent free."

"No," Loki says. "If you're referring to my temple in your tower, you should know that I don't live there, exactly. Not since Ramisiel moved in. I was not in at the time, and, well, I see no reason to return."

Vivienne takes an involuntary half-step forward. "You know about—?"

Ruby stops her with a tug of the chain and a warning look, then smiles brightly again.

"Yes, darling," she says. "I know you said the bastard wasn't your problem, but you are the one who let him in. And that's not to mention the fact that a great many of your things are still there. Priceless things. Powerful things—"

"True," Loki says. "I do love my things."

"And without those things, you won't be able to fully manifest on my side of the Coil anymore. You'll be left with only these power-draining temporary fuck portals and the dubious services of various avatars, all things that regularly leave you somewhat ... less than satisfied."

"So the two of you are here promising to satisfy me?" Loki asks then, pushing away a lithe young blonde boy in their lap as they lean forward to nip at the inside of Ruby's knee.

"Not if you don't help us get the demon out of my building, we won't." Ruby rakes her nails across Loki's scalp in a gesture that further musses the god's already-tousled hair.

"You do drive a hard bargain, Ms. Killingsworth," Loki says, nuzzling their temple against Ruby's knee as they run their fingers up the outside of her calf. "I am once again feeling inclined to acquiesce to your conditions."

Vivienne bites her lower lip. Ruby seems to be handling this pretty well on her own. Other than the transport and the thing with the bouncer, she could have done this whole deal herself. So why's Vivienne there? Muscle? Convenience? Get the introduction handled, call that invoice paid, and be done with whatever was between them for good?

Maybe it doesn't matter. Vivienne's whole life will be better if this is the last she ever sees of Ruby Killingsworth. But since when has she ever wanted what's good for her? She shakes her head and tries not to think too hard. Get through tonight and let the future handle itself ...

The show is just finishing up on the stage with a colorful musical blow-out, and Loki offers gentle, languid applause for the performance. On cue, so do their many lovers, who clap, whistle, and shout their endorsement.

"So you'll agree to help us," Ruby says. "Out of your own self-interest, as per usual."

"I suppose," they say. "Do the thing for the mortal, get the thing from the mortal, enjoy some time with the mortal. As you say, per usual."

"And any pact you may have made with Ramisiel is null and void?"

Loki's eyes glitter like cut emeralds. "Agreed." That velvet voice teases along Vivienne's ears. "And maybe a little prelude, since we're all here?"

"Of course, darling." Ruby smirks. "You didn't really think I'd pass up that chance?"

Loki gestures, and abruptly their attendants stop what they're doing and shake their heads as though coming out of some sort of dream. They look around, confused, and several angry gazes settle on the two interlopers. Vivienne tenses, ready for an attack—this must be why Ruby brought her—but instead they just wander off, most of them remembering to adjust their clothes back into place, all of them pulling out phones that instantly absorb their attention. Based on her previous experiences with live theatre, the private theater empties out with what can only be divinely inspired efficiency, and the troll bouncer shuts the curtain tightly, leaving just the three of them alone in the warm space, still charged with sex and desire. If anything, Loki becomes even more magnetic now, without anyone to distract the attention.

"Ok," Vivienne says. "So—"

Loki leans back, spreading their arms out wide across the back of the velvet couch. Auburn hair falls around the god's fine cheekbones and across their mostly bare chest. They spread their legs and smile, as if waiting for a different sort of show.

"Oh," Vivienne says. "So, I was half right."

"What's that, pet?" Ruby asks, running her fingers through Vivienne's hair to push it behind her ear.

"Oh, nothing." Vivienne lays her hands around Ruby's face and kisses her deeply.

Ruby pulls away for a moment and meets her gaze. "You are all right with this?"

"Boundaries, right?" Vivienne asks.

"Exactly."

"Yes."

"Good."

They kiss for a while and caress, running their fingers over each other's warm skin, then Ruby sinks down to kneel on Loki's velvet sofa. Vivienne gasps, chewing on her lip and grasping Ruby's hand spread across her belly. She chances to meet Loki's eyes, which seem to glow in the semi-darkness. Pleasure coursing through her, she feels herself drawn into the god's world, wolves howling in the distance, and everything feels suddenly cold. Perhaps she imagines it, but she thinks a golden crown appears around Loki's dark brow.

Ultimately, she ends up on the floor, with Loki beckoning, and she crawls toward the god. Ruby has poured herself onto the soft couch beside them, and their lips are locked in an elaborate, elegant dance. Vivienne touches Loki, and it makes her shiver. She has to touch Ruby to keep track of herself, and this seems to have the same effect on Ruby, who looks down, smiles, and lifts Vivienne's chin.

"So it's to be like that, is it?" Vivienne says, though no one had any illusions.

Loki kisses Ruby, making her sigh, and leans down to kiss Vivienne. Their lips meet.

How does she keep getting herself in these situations?

Not that she's complaining.

ROUND FIVE: CHASER

"Definitely femme," Vivienne says, drumming her fingers against the varnished wood of the town car's narrow counter.

"Darling." Ruby shakes her head, the way one might at an enthusiastically mistaken child explaining something they learned incorrectly in school that day. "As enthusiastically as I support lady-dicks in general, most of those moves were far more masc than femme."

"Did ... did you just say lady-dick?"

Ruby straightens up, annoyed. "And what's wrong with that?"

"Language, Miss Killingsworth," Vivienne says. "I thought you'd call it something like, I dunno, femme-phallus."

"What?" Ruby blinks at her. "Don't be gauche."

Vivienne grins. "I am rubbing off on you, aren't I?"

"Business before pleasure, darling."

Once again, they table the ongoing debate as to Loki's gender expression at the time of their very memorable ménage à trois. It's gone on at least a week now, with Vivienne stubbornly and incorrectly insisting Loki went more femme than masc that night, and Ruby pretending she's not out of her mind.

She's enjoyed a rendezvous with Loki on numerous occasions and suspects the trickster god did this on purpose. It really would be just like Loki to give the two of them completely dissimilar, albethey simultaneous, experiences.

Ruby puts her opera glasses to her eyes to check out the tower across the way through the mirrored windows of the limousine they'd spent most of the afternoon camped out in.

Still nothing.

The city very helpfully declared the demon-infested building "under construction" and posted "hazardous chemicals" signs, and

81

she has so far fended off reporters trying to get the lowdown on what's been happening there. To her knowledge, the tower is completely abandoned, and it's starting to look the part: the windows haven't been cleaned, the lawns are overgrown, the plants dead, and most of the lights are flickering or not coming on at all. Just her luck. One little demon comes along, and her beautiful tower that she invested so much time and money into becomes some haunted ruin festering like a cancerous sore in the middle of Cobalt City.

"Where is that damned Loki?" Ruby asks, letting her frustration slip free of her restraint. "I swear, you and your girlfriend give a Norse god the greatest night of his eternity, and he doesn't even call."

"You think we were better than the horse?" Vivienne asks.

"What?" Ruby isn't used to other people being around when she mutters in frustration.

"You know, the horse." Vivienne is drinking from a black and silver flask. "Odin's horse. Sleipnir. Only not him, but his father. Uh, horse-father."

"Svaðilfari." Ruby reaches over and takes the flask away. She needs Vivienne sober. "And yes, we were better than the damn horse."

"Cool." Vivienne drums her clawed fingers on the deep crimson leather of Ruby's limo's generous backseat. "Also, did you just call me your girlfriend?"

"What? Obviously not."

"I'm pretty sure you did."

"Slip of the tongue, darling."

"I'll bet."

Ruby's in a terrible mood. Today started off with a massive indignity. Vivienne convinced her to fly on a commercial service, rather than her private jet. Something about absorbing power on the flight, but after six hours of sub-par champagne and other people, Ruby isn't sure it was worth it.

But honestly, Vivienne has come back to Cobalt City against her stringent objections, and for that, Ruby can endure a little indignity.

"Loki's going to do the heavy lifting, right?" Vivienne asks.

"That's the plan."

"She's not going to betray us?"

"You heard him," Ruby says. "Any pact he may have made with Ramisiel is null and void."

"All right," Vivienne bites her lip. "Because I told you I'm not powerful enough without—"

"We made a pact and sealed it with ... well not blood, but you know."

"Right."

Ruby's stomach rumbles, but she suppresses the embarrassing sound as best she can. It's late enough in the day, and the travel stress has gotten to her enough, that she really ought to have eaten by now. She has exhausted the limo's supply of almonds, carrot sticks, and hummus, all to no avail. They're down to the champagne, vodka, and whiskey, which she carefully locked up to make sure Vivienne can't get at it and drink her powers away.

"Sooo—" Vivienne drags out the word, clearly trying to work through her nerves. "Hottest person you've ever slept with. Other than Loki."

"Man or woman, either or both?"

"Let's go with the boys."

"Other than Jaccob?"

"Please."

Ruby casts her mind back. So many men, so many options. Mostly, the issue is remembering names.

"There was this Italian speed skater—Frederico, I think his name was?"

"Was he a cape?"

"Nope, just really, really fast," Ruby says with a little smile. "Well, at most things."

"Nice."

Ruby enjoys the taste of the memory. "How about you?"

"Antonio DeSantes," Vivienne says. "The Raven."

"Of course," Ruby says. "That man is very attractive. Intense. Dangerous. I can see the appeal."

"Mm-hmm."

"Didn't he spend the last few years trying to murder you? After you gouged his eye out?"

"And your point is?"

"Fair." Ruby inspects the tower again—still nothing—and passes the glasses to Vivienne. "You two were in Supergroup together, right? Was he—?"

"My first?" Vivienne checks out the tower. "I was sixteen, he was seventeen. Obviously."

"Aww." Ruby forces the approval a little, though honestly, it sounds pretty adorable. "Teenage sweethearts, how precious."

"Oh no, that was just sex. And oof, it was good sex. Not just in that 'I'm sixteen and don't know what good sex is' way. Just really good." She gives a wicked little smile. "He's only gotten better at it, too."

"Ok, ok, forget I asked."

"How about you, Goblin Queen? Who was your first love?" Vivienne gives her a sidelong look. "And don't do that tough girl thing where you say you've never loved anyone."

"I told you never to use that word in my presence."

"Come on, Highness," Vivienne says, "be human for a moment. Feelings. You've had them. You don't want me to use the word? Fine? But the question stands."

Ruby pauses, she's oddly thoughtful for a moment, then she sighs. "I'm honestly not sure I have. Come close a few times, but I don't think I could tell you which was the first."

"That's not really the kind of thing a person forgets."

"It is when you have lots of magic and a very strong desire to purge such things from memory. All those people who try to tell you pain and suffering build character are full of bull. They only say those things to justify trauma they can't let go of. Well I can, and I have. I don't need that energy in my world thankyouverymuch."

"Okay, fair." It isn't really. What Vivienne wouldn't give for the ability to scrub her brain of past heartbreaks. But at least Ruby's being honest, and it's not like she can blame her.

"Ok." Ruby shrugs. "So who was the first person you ever … you know?"

There's a pause, and Vivienne ultimately sighs. "The Shrike."

"Ew." Ruby makes a face. "Age is just a number, but isn't he seventy? And in prison?"

"I mean the *second* Shrike. His kid."

"I see." Ruby nods. "Man or woman?"

"Yes."

"Ooh." Ruby is suddenly less interested in the stakeout. "Well, come on. Details."

Vivienne is looking out the window, her expression … wistful. "I don't really want to talk about it."

"You brought it up," Ruby says. "What, were they that bad?"

"The opposite." Vivienne sighs again. "And I don't mean sex. We never got that far. But Wren was the first person I ever really fell for. And I fucked that up. Hard."

"By—?"

"Cheating," Vivienne says. "With Tony. Again."

"Yikes."

"Well, that's what happens when you're a big hot mess." She gropes about for a glass and has to settle for a bottle of water. She grimaces. "So ... if you don't remember the first person, how about the best person you ever had those feelings ... or ... *almost* had those feelings for, as the case may be?"

"The *best* person?" Ruby asks, which is mostly a way to deflect the question. She knows the answer immediately. "I mean, how do you measure best, anyway—"

"Shit," Vivienne says. "It's Jaccob, isn't it?"

"What?" Ruby turns away to hide her flush. "I didn't say that. Why would you think—?" She looks back to Vivienne, who is giving her a sympathetic look. "Oh, shut up, you big hot mess."

~

By three o'clock, with still no sign of their immortal co-conspirator, they order in. Vivienne is a little bit amazed by the revelation a person can order a pizza delivered to a parked limousine, but she is beginning to learn that, with enough money, pretty much anything is possible.

"This is supposed to be authentic Chicago-style deep dish pizza?" Ruby looks unconvinced.

"How would I know?" Vivienne says. "I've never even been to Chicago. Just try it, Princess."

"You know I don't eat carbs."

"You know I don't give a damn. You need to eat something. We both do. There is a pizza in front of us and we're going to eat the goddamned pizza. Or did you want me to eat all of it?"

Vivienne dives in without a second thought. Ruby hesitates, but not for long. Vivienne is right that she needs to eat something; there's no telling what magics she'll need once they get inside. She may need all the strength she can get, in which case a little protein wouldn't hurt. She chooses the smallest slice and begins to nibble.

"This is a travesty," Ruby says, just a few bites in. "A miscarriage of justice."

"Now you're all of the sudden an expert on pizza, Miss I don't eat Carbsingworth?"

"One, that was terrible. Two, I will have you know that in my life I have eaten many a pizza in the city of Chicago, and I can assure you this is not it."

"Louisiana to Chicago is a long way," Vivienne says. Ruby is usually less-than-forthcoming about anything that happened in pre-billionaire life. And when Vivienne sees an in, she decides to take it.

"I happen to have spent my teen years in Detroit." Ruby picks at the pizza with her polished green fingernails. "And when you're a teenager in Detroit, Chicago is where you run away to when you're bored and want a change of scenery."

"Ah, middle America." Vivienne takes another bite of the perfectly appetizing pizza and smiles. "Let me guess, Friday Night Lights and all that went with it?"

"Do I really give off cheerleader energy?"

"I think I'd like to see you in a little pleated skirt."

"As much as I don't blame you for the fantasy—" Ruby snickers. She frees a sliver of green pepper from its cheesy prison and pops it into her mouth. "—real life was quite the opposite. High school was dull, the people were duller. When I bothered to show up at all it was for the free music lessons and the chance to play in the pit when the school put on a show. Mostly I played hooky to make music elsewhere."

"Wait." Vivienne is stunned. Somehow it hadn't ever occurred to her to wonder how it was Ruby got to where she is. Ruby likes to act like she emerged from the womb a fully formed CEO. This is the first Vivienne has heard of tales from the before times, Frederico the speed skater notwithstanding. "You started in the business as a musician?"

"A recording artist," Ruby says, her tone as casual as if commenting on the color of her shoes. She's looking out the window, licking sauce off her fingers when she adds, "Teen idol, if you'd believe it."

"You were what?" Vivienne can't believe what she's hearing. She searches her memory for any since-vanished teen pop star from her youth. She isn't altogether sure how old Ruby is, but there are only so many years of possibility. When the answer comes to her, she nearly chokes on pizza crust. "Wait—you're—"

"Don't you dare say it." Ruby turns her head to glower.

Vivienne is sure she feels magic behind that order. "Holy shit," she says, instead of the name that's on the tip of her tongue.

"Well, now you know all my secrets, don't you?" Ruby turns back to look out the window.

"I am sure I don't."

"You're right, you don't."

"But holy shit!"

"All right, Captain Pleated Skirt, so what were you like in high school?" Ruby smirks as she plucks a mushroom from the pizza.

"Demon-possessed."

"Oh, that's right." Against her better judgment, Ruby takes an actual bite of the slice of pizza she's been picking at for several minutes. Might as well commit at this point. "But what about after that? When you were with that young heroes group, what was it? Awesome Agents?"

"Agents of Awesome. And I was about what you'd expect. Rebellious. Slutty. Always hungover. A real bitch most of the time."

"I can definitely imagine that. But you were just a kid, right? You couldn't have done anything that bad—"

"I cheated on the Shrike and broke up the team, after I sealed the demon lord Azazel inside a creepy dude and locked him in his basement and burned his house down."

"I stand corrected."

Vivienne said it so flippantly, like a joke, but Ruby heard the pain in her voice. That must have been twenty, twenty-five years ago, and she's still hurting about it? Ruby can't even imagine regretting something that much, but Vivienne definitely feels it, and that makes her ... a little uncomfortable. Like she needs to sneeze but can't.

"Listen, V—"

"We've got movement," Vivienne says, gazing out the window with the opera glasses. She hands them over to Ruby.

"About damn time," Ruby says, taking a look for herself. "It was a pain in my whole ass setting up enough foci to get him out here without needing an Avatar. The least he could have done was try and be punctual."

"Did she tell you why she wanted to use the front door instead of manifesting in her own space?"

"Why the hell does he do anything? Probably just to make things a slightly bigger pain in the ass for me."

"But you cooperate."

"So he'll cooperate."

"No wonder the two of you are such a riot in bed."

"I didn't hear you complaining."

"And you won't."

Sure enough, Loki approaches the building. He doesn't look the same as last time, obviously, but Ruby knows it's him with just a glance at that damnably confident swagger. He's gone full Bowie for the occasion, complete with robe-length jacket, a massive green feather boa, and gold-rimmed aviator sunglasses. He's such a showboat.

"Time to get ready," Ruby says, handing the glasses back so she can gather her things. That and condemn the rest of the awful "pizza" to the trash.

Tangentially, Ruby wonders why she keeps thinking of the incredibly genderfluid Loki as "he" and "him," and wonders what that says about her own pansexuality. Vivienne seems to be into a wide spectrum of lovers, but perhaps she's a bit more into the feminine than the masculine? In which case, Ruby supposes she's on the winning side of things—although she did only spend a few minutes on her hair this morning ...

Stop it, Ruby Killingsworth, she tells herself. You're a sorceress in charge of a multibillion-dollar corporation, not some schoolgirl with a crush.

"You say something, Your Worship?" Vivienne, peering through the binoculars at Loki, has managed to sneak a bottle of scotch from somewhere and has stuck it between her legs while her non-spyglass holding hand works on breaking the seal. It looks so natural and casual, Ruby suspects Vivienne doesn't even realize she's doing it.

"No." Ruby takes the scotch away, meaning to put it in the limo trash, looks at the label, then puts it in her purse instead. "Focus. We're on."

~

88

The first time Vivienne entered the Goblin Records corporate tower, it struck her with its power and majesty. It was a place of organized, cleverly orchestrated control, where everything had its proper place, and all things were put away. It was the province of a queen who exercised her will over everyone and every particular.

The last time, it was a temple of corporate ascendancy, a shrine to capitalism and all it can create. Gleaming brass fixtures and red velvet carpet stacked to the rafters with everything for sale and filled to capacity with eager teens and their parents, all ready to part with their hard-earned dollars. It was a place teeming with vibrance and possibility, which had barely covered the fear and horror of Ramisiel's influence.

But today it resembles neither.

The once-opulent Ruby Tower now is an utterly alien entity, which Vivienne realizes before they even get inside. She wonders how Ruby is feeling, seeing her beloved palace in such a state, but doesn't dare ask.

The doors are darkened with fog, the light blocked by something thick and dark on the inside of the glass. Vivienne reaches out to pull one of the doors open with her clawed left hand, letting out a wave of hot, muggy air. Ropy vegetation hangs on the inside of the doors, the vines like pulsing veins burrowing into the metal and stretched taut across the glass. The roots twitch slightly away from them, as if with a mind of their own.

"Lovely," Ruby says. "This will cost a fortune in cleaning bills."

"Salt water," Vivienne says, "blessed by a priest, if possible."

"I can't tell if you're joking."

There's power in this place, contained within the bounds of these doors like some sort of magical circle, radiating through the glove. Clicking the barbed fingers, Vivienne looks down to see if there's a salt circle on the pavement. But no, the power is trapped here only because it chooses to be.

"You feel it, too?" Ruby asks.

"The demon's staying here because it wants to," Vivienne says. "It's feeding on something. Or it's waiting for us. Or both."

"Great," Ruby says.

They head inside.

The ground-level lobby is much the same as the front doors: a humid swamp crisscrossed by roots and vines that pulse with malevolence. Sweat breaks out on Vivienne's neck almost instantly.

The electronics crackle, some still functioning, but much of them rendered inoperable.

"Is there an OGP in there that Ramisiel might be interested in?"

"OGP?"

"Object of great power."

"Ah." Ruby purses her lips. "How much time have you got?"

"Great."

"And suddenly, I'm no longer as mad about losing the Eye of Africa on a metaplane," Ruby says under her breath.

"The what?"

"Never mind."

"Your vintage copy of *Romancing the Stone* on VHS?"

Ruby puffs up, offended. "What am I, sixty?"

"You're making a mental note to hide your VHS collection, aren't you?"

"It's back at the house, and you'll never find it."

"Just you wait," Vivienne says. "One of these days, I'll just sneak out of bed in the middle of the night, and I won't come back until I've cataloged every single incriminating tape."

"I could just not have sex with you ever again."

As unlikely as they both know that is, Vivienne stops pushing it. The banter is helping keep them both calm, and while Vivienne can't feel Ruby's fear through the emotional dampening magic, she knows Ruby well enough to recognize her specific signs. Pupils slightly dilated, sweating, quicker breaths—all that is pretty standard. But when Ruby's afraid, there's a certain electric charge around her. Her hair frizzes, not just from the humidity, and her skin tingles. That and the smell of burnt ozone, which is definitely a remnant of some sort of magic. This woman has held great power more than once in her life, and not a small part of Vivienne would like to see her do so again. Not, of course, that Ruby is the sort of woman one should trust with world-shattering power.

Vivienne almost takes Ruby's hand but thinks better of it. Odds are that would just annoy her, and without direct access to her emotions, Vivienne isn't going to take that risk. The stakes are too high. They need to deal with the matter at hand before Vivienne can start dwelling on other matters and other hands.

The lights flicker as they enter, coming on with a whining buzz, then winking out in unpredictable sequences. Music pipes in from unseen speakers, distorted and warbling upbeat pop music that keeps skipping and rebooting in a way that sounds more than vaguely sinister.

"I've never heard the Young Dudes like that," Vivienne says. "Creepy."

Ruby says nothing. That was an attempt to ground her—to remind her that the creepy music is just music that she produced—but it doesn't seem to have worked. Damn.

Not that Vivienne can blame her. The tower's radical transformation is as much psychic as physical. The screens that showed constant streams of Goblin Records bands are still on, but the artists in the videos have taken on a sinister aspect—their eyes too big, their smiles too wide—and every one of them seems to be singing directly at her. The music glitches repeatedly; it slows or picks up the pace unexpectedly, changes the pitch, stutters, and otherwise becomes discordant and wrong in a way that makes Vivienne's teeth grind. The lights hum loudly, buzzing like bug-zappers luring them in.

Eyes gently closing, Vivienne splays out her clawed fingers and rests her palm on the surface of the giant customer service desk halfway between the front doors and the staircase. Purple fire stirs around her hand.

"What are you doing?" Ruby asks in a whisper.

"Getting a feel for what we're up against. And you don't need to whisper. The demon already knows we're here."

"Fantastic. Though Loki should be distracting it."

"If she's doing her part."

"Have a little faith, Goth Girl." Ruby crosses her arms. "Anything? On your ... demon radar, or whatever?"

"Too much." Vivienne frowns. She hears haunting laughter in the back of her head, and it's not just her own resident echo of a demon lord. Shadows lurk around every corner, and she can almost feel the building breathing. She has to remind herself that the pulse beating in her head is her own, and not the tower's. "You sure this place is empty? Of people, I mean."

"It damn well better be," Ruby scoffs. "I'm paying for temporary office space for half a dozen corporate tenants and put all the residents up in very nice hotels. I did most of that before you showed up the first time, remember?"

"Sure."

There may be no one here, but the building doesn't *feel* empty. The demon's power has leaked down from the penthouse and infested the whole place with an army of consciousness. Vivienne has learned a fair bit about demons, since the first time she was possessed as a thirteen-year-old girl, but she hardly knows everything. Is this just one demon—Ramisiel—or has he conjured an army up from whatever Hell dimension he came from?

"If it were Azazel," Vivienne says, "I'd know exactly what was going on, but Rami is a bit... opaque."

"Rammy?" Ruby asks. "I didn't realize you were on a pet name basis."

"Don't get all jealous on me. Any demon would be just as happy to shove *your* soul into the back closet and wear your skin like a pantsuit so he can go torture and kill everyone you love. While you sit there, in the back of your own mind, screaming and begging him to stop."

"That—that's what possession's like? I thought—I thought you were just asleep or something."

"Nope. No, you get to be awake the whole time. It's pretty fucking traumatic. If you're lucky, you'll manage to hold onto your sanity, dignity, and/or self-respect."

"And if you're not?"

It's all Vivienne can do not to gesture to herself. Self-pity isn't a trait she likes about herself. She pulls her hand away, ripping free the threads of purple flame that connect her claws to the polished stone. She wasn't aware of pushing down, but deep grooves in the desk show that she cut into it with the claws.

"Sorry about that, Princess," she says. "Uh—?"

Ruby is just standing there, staring past the desk at the retail elevator's hammered brass doors, which are overgrown with demonic vines. And while she doesn't feel anything emanating from the sorceress—nothing can pierce the protective barrier she magically erected around her emotions—Vivienne can certainly see the effects on her. She breathes shallowly, and her jugular thuds particularly hard.

Subtly, Vivienne reaches down with her ungloved hand and takes Ruby's hand. That snaps her out of it—that gentle touch.

"Excuse me," Ruby says. "What are you doing?"

"It's ok to be afraid," Vivienne says.

"Afraid." Ruby scoffs, though it's only halfway convincing. "I'm not afraid."

"Your hands are trembling."

"They are not."

"And you're sweating."

"A lady does not sweat. But I may be glistening ... a little. I'm glad I wore my hair up, anyway. "

"I can feel your pulse, Ginger. You're either scared, or you're really excited to hold my hand."

"That's ridiculous." Now Ruby sounds insulted, and she scrunches up her face in disgust. "Besides, I've done far more than hold your hand, darling."

"Yeah, but have you ever actually held my hand?"

"Oh, you can fuck right off, Mascara Waterfall. Hand-holding is just not my speed."

"Fine." Vivienne loosens her grip, but Ruby tightens hers, restraining her hand in place.

"I didn't say let go."

Vivienne smiles wryly and squeezes Ruby's hand reassuringly. Tough as she is, Ruby doesn't protest. In fact, as they approach the elevator, the sorceress edges a little closer.

"Are you quite sure we should be using this?" Ruby asks. "It's just that I've seen horror movies about elevators. And episode 1.7 of *The X-Files*."

"It's fine." Vivienne hopes it's true. She pushes the elevator call button. "So long as we stick together, Ramisiel can't just kill us. He needs one of us—preferably you, I think."

"Why me?"

"Why not? Look at this place. Look at your bank account. You've got the leader of the free world at your beck and call, when you can stand dealing with the greasy shitweasel. Not to mention all that magical power you're carting around. You're rich, powerful, and beautiful."

"Oh, stop it. I mean, do go on, of course."

"Not to mention that you're white, and you're much better at covering up your scandals." Vivienne smirks. "What, is Ramisiel going to go with burnt-out, used-up, old me? Fuck, *I* wouldn't settle for me if I had the choice."

"That's not—" Ruby trails off and looks awkward.

"What? Were you just going to compliment me or something? Shit, I want to hear this."

Ruby rolls her eyes. "Oh, let's just get this over with."

Privately, Vivienne smiles in triumph. A little flattery and banter, and Ruby doesn't seem as afraid anymore. That's good. They're going to need her on her game when they get up to her office.

Also, Vivienne avoided mentioning that Ramisiel wouldn't want to shit in Azazel's bed. The Many-Mouthed Devourer has claimed her more than once, and no matter how much she denies it, every step into this tower convinces her more that she belongs to him.

He's been unexpectedly quiet, thus far. A blessing, or a warning?

She'll be careful.

The elevator dings and they step inside.

~

If there's one thing Ruby Killingsworth hates most in the world—well, there are about a hundred things she hates most in the world—but definitely among the top ten is having to rely on someone else. Closely followed by *seeming* to have to rely on someone else, and also being vulnerable.

Ruby Killingsworth does not *do* vulnerable.

Since she was a teenager ... no, before that, since she was ten years old, and her new stepfather failed to keep a simple promise regarding a gift, she has done everything she could possibly do to avoid having to depend on anyone. People, in her experience, are unreliable.

Generally, she finds manipulation the most effective way of getting what she wants from people. Compulsion and coercion work in a pinch, but over the long term, it breeds resentment and bad blood, making it a zero-sum strategy at best. The best way to get someone to give her what she wants, she has found over and over, is to give them what they want. To make them believe it's their idea, because it *is*. She has always preferred the carrot to the stick.

Vivienne Cain, however, she cannot seem to lead around by the nose.

Clearly the woman needs money. Ruby's accountants have determined Vivienne has significant debts, an abysmal credit score, and that isn't even counting the recent destruction and rebuild of her place of business in Seattle. But for whatever reason, it never seems to matter all that much to her. At best, she accepts Ruby's generosity, though she never seems to see it as transactional. All of this would be much easier if Vivienne would just get in her pocket like a good minion, but she infuriatingly refuses to do so.

Though really, wouldn't Ruby rather have Vivienne in her *pants*?

"Now is *not* the time," she says under her breath. "Figure out your complicated sex life after you exorcise your building."

"Did you say something?" Vivienne asks.

Ruby meant to keep that inside her head, and the fact she didn't does not bode well. "Not at all."

The elevator has lifted them about halfway to their destination. It shakes and judders, but at least it's still operational. Through the cracked glass, Ruby sees thick, low clouds rolling in to hide Cobalt City. Rarely has she ever felt quite so isolated and quite so vulnerable at the same time, neither of which she enjoys.

"You feel anything?" Vivienne asks.

"Trepidation and annoyance."

"I mean anything magical."

"You told me not to."

"Yeah, but that doesn't mean you didn't."

"Ugh. No faith. No faith at all."

Indeed, Ruby focuses on her subtle sensor spell, letting it relay information to her mentally and empathically. As soon as they entered the building, she renewed her connection with it, allowing her to feel every floor and window, to detect the entities within and get a sense of their state. Vivienne hadn't wanted her to do that, as the demon could get at her too easily if its influence had sunk too deep into the building, but if her magic could keep out Vivienne's empathic invocation, it should be able to protect her from a demon.

This place is hers. Her sanctum. No one claims it but her. She willed this place into being, and she'll be damned if some extradimensional trespasser tramples over her connection to it.

That said, Ruby can definitely feel what Vivienne was talking about. Ramisiel's will has permeated the building, seeping like blood into a sponge left to soak in it. Those first few days, the demon probably hadn't exerted any sort of grip on the tower, but now she feels its presence as if it's looming over her, breathing huskily on her neck, its gross, oily presence impossible to ignore.

Perhaps Vivienne was right to warn her off reactivating her empathic connection. Not that Ruby could ever tell her.

"We're almost up to Loki's sanctum," Ruby says. "You can feel him, right?"

"Yes, she's definitely there. Hopefully doing her fucking job."

"Well, if you can say anything for Loki, it's that he's good at fucking jobs."

"Heh."

Ruby can feel the God of Mischief too, through the way his magic always flavored her own when he was in the building. She had to build a special exception into her wards to allow him to abide in the tower, and she feels it like a numb spot in her awareness. Not entirely empty, but tingling, like a phantom limb. She isn't sure if Loki knows about the partial exemption, or whether he thinks she just took the much easier route of simply not enchanting his bachelor pad. Probably he knows and doesn't care, but if he's underestimated her, it wouldn't be the first time.

For most of her life, Ruby hadn't been a particularly powerful sorceress. It was from those limitations that she'd grown to be *damn* meticulous. Sculpting the wards on this building had taken a year of work, both before and after she'd lost and regained her use of magic. She'd made the arcane web in and around and over this building absolutely flawless. And Ramisiel is *fucking* with it ...

"Still using he for Loki, huh? That's neat."

Ruby groans. "Isn't this what we were talking about in the car?"

"Were we? I don't remember."

She definitely does, Ruby knows it, but she's making an effort to keep it light—keep the tension down. In another life, Vivienne could be a pretty good psychologist. At least, if she were a little more subtle.

The doors ding open at the office level, which is an overgrown mess of vine-wrapped furniture, scattered papers, and malfunctioning screens. And it only gets worse as they traverse the public areas and enter the C-suite. Ruby's own office is perhaps the worst of all: practically a maze of vines and tendrils, some of which hang from the ceiling and twist like snakes. Her beautiful desk of reclaimed wood, which had so impressed Vivienne the first day they met, is stained with demonic goo. One more reason to punch Ramisiel in every single dick limb she can reach.

The good news is there's no demonic presence up here—at least, no more than anywhere else in the building. A realization Vivienne confirms with a slight nod.

"Well, Loki must be distracting Rami," Vivienne says. "We have some time. Can you access your locus or not?"

"Keep your knickers on, darling."

"Bold of you to assume I wear those."

"We've been over this."

"Yeah, but you don't know about *today*."

Ruby moves to the center of the massive office, just behind the wrecked desk. There, she spreads her hands, intones the ritual, and falls into her magic. Sure enough, she's able to connect, a process she began down in the lobby, and because she put in all that early work, it has saved her time up here.

She feels the demonic presence much more objectively here, like oil coating her exposed skin. She starts sweating. "This feels really disgusting."

"Well, you're crossing a demon," Vivienne says. "If it doesn't feel a bit like having shitty sex while covered in tree sap, you're doing something wrong."

"Thanks for that." Ruby scowls.

This is the most dangerous part, Vivienne told her—tapping into the building's locus of control to expunge the demonic taint. It's like that old Nietzsche quote the goth kids used when she was young—something about staring into an abyss, and how if you don't watch your back, someone will push you in.

A screeching sound disturbs Ruby, and she looks up sharply.

"Sorry." Vivienne shrugs, and goes back to tracing symbols in the marble of Ruby's office floor.

"Are you quite sure that's really necessary?" Ruby asks. "You would throw up if you knew how much that stone cost."

"What, is it crushed up blood diamonds or something?"

"It contains veins of fossilized ivory, if you must know."

Vivienne rolls her eyes.

"Oh sure. Judge me."

Ruby intones invocations she spent last night studying based on rituals performed by Elias Cortés, inquisitor and exorcist of 700 years ago. Cortés, according to her research, had driven a dozen demons and one apparent angel out of his fellow inquisitors, though he'd never actually found a confirmed case of possession among the hundreds of innocent women he'd had put to death. His rituals were rough and full of useless prayer and exhortations to divine entities, but she'd been able to distill them easily enough to get to the useful stuff. Each one of those invocations feels like a sweep of a broom pushing back a flow of muck seeping over the floor of her beautiful tower. A morass of half-rotted roots riddled with maggots, like a psychic fungus growing throughout her tower. Ick.

"Progress?" Vivienne asks.

"Darling. It's me."

Ruby wishes she were quite as confident as she made it sound. The problem, however, is that a broom is the wrong tool for cleaning up mud. It tends to pick up as much mud as it pushes out of the way. Soon enough, her rituals are corrupted and soured by touching the demonic taint, and she's just moving filth around.

"Ok, I need you," Ruby says at length.

She's almost hoping Vivienne responds with something like "What? Here?", but it seems every bit of humor has drained out of her. She has drawn several wards between the desk and the walls and windows—five in total, creating a pentagram in Ruby's office. As a more modern pagan, Ruby's never gone in for the traditional witchy stuff, but the classics are sometimes the best, and the pentagram is a very stable protective structure. When Ramisiel comes for them, Vivienne's magic will slow it, or even stop it entirely. Between all the fear energy she picked up on the flight over and the power of that glove, she's got this.

Right?

"Here we go," Vivienne says, and traces lines of power in the air. Abruptly, the filth Ruby has collected with her cleaning spell slops off, falling into what is, best Ruby can figure, a pocket dimension.

"So, where is this going?" she asks.

"The Fearworld." Vivienne is sweating. "I'll tell you about it sometime."

"Sounds like a terrible vacation spot."

"You have no idea."

That particular artifact, her claw, is one that Ruby wouldn't mind examining at some point. Apparently she got it from a D-tier demonologist when she was a teen, but Ruby can't imagine said practitioner was using it to its full potential. Vivienne herself only seems to be using it in a truncated fashion. What Ruby could do with that claw ...

No. That was Ramisiel trying to influence her. Promising power, secrets, and control.

The demon knows they're here. She has to work faster.

As if on cue, the elevator whirs to life and heads down. Vivienne flinches toward it and hits the call button, but to no avail.

"We're running out of time," Vivienne says. "How's it going?"

"I'm about halfway there. I think."

"Great." Vivienne flexes her fingers in the glove and positions herself between the desk and the elevator. She cleans Ruby's purging spell again, though not all the demon scum comes out of it. Her magic feels darker and smells like something rotting.

Ruby catches her breath. They settled on this arrangement of duties because she had the connection with the tower, even though Vivienne was definitely the more experienced exorcist. Also, Ruby's magic wasn't exactly what you'd call attuned to combat, so Vivienne was better qualified for fighting Ramisiel if—*when*—it came to that. Still, Ruby didn't want either of them to be here. She should just stop. Abandon this place. Run away.

"*No*," Ruby says. "That shit might work on some people, but my will is stronger than that."

The demon seems displeased, which she takes as a good sign.

The elevator starts whirring again. It was a pretty short trip. Which is much less reassuring.

"The fuck," Vivienne says. "I thought Loki would have kept Rami busy at least a few more minutes. What are they doing down there?"

"Pretty sure," Ruby says through gritted teeth, "we don't want to know."

"Hard agree."

It's becoming much, much more difficult. The more Ruby shoves at the taint, the more she feels like she's just spreading it around. Not only is it all over the floors and walls, but it's on her hands and her feet. She can feel it tingling over her skin like filth left to fester. She wants Vivienne to cleanse her magic again, even now, only a couple minutes later, but she knows the woman needs to reserve her magic for the impending battle. She thought this would be easier. She thought they would have more time. She thought ...

Ruby knuckles under the despair and shoves harder, thrusting her will with greater force against the corruption in the tower. She's got most of it, she realizes, but the remaining roots are tenacious. And far removed. She can't reach them all, not without letting some others wriggle free of her magic. She needs to purge her exorcism spell again.

"V," she says. "V, I need—"

The elevator dings. Ruby stiffens. Vivienne braces.

The figure that emerges isn't one either of them expect. Dressed in an impeccable green suit, they are tall, lithe, and handsome as hell, with chiseled features and a sardonic smile. Loki Laufeyson defies labels or categorization—they are simply them, now as always.

"What," Vivienne says. "Did ... did you kill it?"

"You awful son of a bitch." Ruby feels the demon approaching. "You betrayed us."

Vivienne doesn't waste time on accusations. She lunges toward Loki, clawed hand slashing, but tendrils of dark filth burst free of the ivory tile of the floor and smash her upward with shattering force into the high ceiling. There they hold her, wrapping her limbs in their squirming, coursing coils. She would be cursing up a storm if she could breathe.

Ramisiel seeps out of the cracks in the tile, an amorphous blob that takes on a shape vaguely reminiscent of a willow tree, but with countless red berries like eyes and knotholes that turn into mouths. It utters a chuckle in a dozen discordant voices.

"My dears." Loki spreads their hands and smiles wider. "I do appreciate our time together, but I simply received a better offer I am quite certain I mentioned."

"I'll bet you did," Ruby says, sweat pouring down her forehead.

If Loki wanted to strike her down, this would be a perfect opportunity to do it, but the God of Mischief doesn't. Instead, he crosses over to the one remaining piece of intact furniture in the room—a red leather divan—and drapes himself over it. A tumbler of what looks like whiskey comes from nowhere, and Loki lounges to watch.

"You—" Ruby calls to mind the invocation of a slaying spell—not her forte, but no self-respecting sorceress doesn't know how to kill an irritating pissant with magic—but a cry from above stays her hand.

Vivienne falls with a crunch to the floor, covered in demon blood where she cut herself free, using that sword of purple fire in her hand.

Ramisiel hisses at her, tendrils whipping all around its amorphous form.

"Keep working," Vivienne says over her shoulder to Ruby, blood trickling from the corner of her mouth. "I'll handle this."

"Oh, wonderful." Loki applauds.

Anger fills Ruby, but she knows Loki well enough to know the score. Perhaps he sold the women out, but the pact didn't include killing them. They still have a chance.

As Vivienne engages the creature, slashing at its tentacles from every direction, Ruby refocuses her efforts on her ritual. Vivienne is right. Interrupting it now would destroy all their efforts.

Ramisiel's physical presence in the room with them stabs into her awareness like a spike, but the creature's influence elsewhere in the tower is weak and diffuse. Ruby sends her magic lancing out, seeking those last vestiges, but some of the darkness clinging to her slithers free. It's like trying to pick up too many things, or, better, like trying to reach a far table without letting go of the handle of the door to the room. She's stretched too thin, and her magic feels frayed and porous.

Vivienne sets herself firmly like a samurai, blade raised over her head, and brings it down in a series of devastating slashes, bisecting Ramisiel's tentacles with the crunch of chopped vegetables. They spew sap all over, which resembles a mix of blood and pus. It splashes Vivienne, but she wades through, unperturbed, to hack at another mass of tentacles probing along the floor toward Ruby at the center of the room.

"Any time now," Vivienne says, her voice dark and low.

"Better hurry," Loki adds. "Wouldn't want to have to do something drastic."

That makes Vivienne's face go a little paler, and for a second, it seems like she might say something. Instead, she keeps hacking away at seeking tentacles with increasing desperation.

For her part, Ruby isn't paying attention. Maybe if she splits her focus ... no, she's not strong enough to hold the darkness she's claimed or pull back the others, let alone grab all the filth in the

tower. She needs Vivienne to cleanse her magic again, or she can't
...

"Ginger!" Vivienne, teeth gritted, chops with slowing strength, while two more tentacles snake their way around behind her. Their barbs tear at her jeans, her leather jacket, and the skin beneath. Vivienne utters a curse as they tear one of the sleeves off her jacket, casting a disgusting parallel with the thorny vine ink that wraps her arm. She bleeds freely from a dozen wounds, all of them small, but they will add up.

Ruby's heart thuds in her throat, and she realizes that she's paying more attention to the battle than her own magic. She has to figure this out. Because if she doesn't, Vivienne's going to die, probably quite horribly, and she'll be next.

"Dammit." Ruby inverts her incantation, pulling instead of thrusting. The taint drains toward her, as though her magic has suddenly become a vacuum cleaner rather than a broom. First only specks hit her, then globs of demonic filth, and she has to remind herself that it's her magic, not her own body.

"Come on," she says. "Here I am. Take me."

Ramisiel's attention wavers, and its tree trunk head turns toward her. Being the focus of those crimson bulb eyes is one of the most unsettling things Ruby Killingsworth has ever experienced.

"No." Abruptly, a flash of purple energy fills the room, and the tentacles holding Vivienne disintegrate in a mist of blood and darkness. Ramisiel staggers back, screeching in a dozen inhuman voices. Vivienne lands amongst the wreckage, catching herself on her gloved hand. Sprouting from her back is a black and purple wing of pure fear energy. The last of her reserves, and it's only a partial manifestation. What if she channeled enough to have two wings? Or more? She could destroy Ramisiel without trouble.

Is that her own thought? Where did that come from? But there's no time to wonder.

"Yes!" Ruby says as the last of the taint fills her magic. It nearly bursts the limits of her power, but she can hold it. She has to. "V!"

Vivienne, bearing down on the reeling Ramisiel, looks back to Ruby. She seems to understand immediately what needs to happen, and lunges back toward her. The demon reaches out with its many tendrils, trying to pull her back ...

Too late. The claws of Vivienne's gauntlet slash through Ruby's magic, banishing the last of the demon's taint to her Fearworld.

Her purple wing wraps around Ruby to protect her from the rushing magic.

The impact on Ramisiel is instantaneous and comprehensive. The tree-like demon lurches to a halt, turning gray and stone-like. It droops, then crumbles to dust, as do its tentacles reaching all around the room. As the women watch, panting in each other's arms, the veins threading the walls turn ashen and then break apart.

"Good enough show for you, Trickster?" Ruby asks. "Too bad it's over now."

"Hardly," Loki says, inclining his head. "We're just getting to the good part." He dissolves into the air then as though he was never there.

"What—"

But Ruby knows the answer. Slowly, tremulously, she turns to look at Vivienne, who won't meet her eye. "Vivienne?"

The woman finally turns to her, moving a bit stiffly, and Ruby's stomach turns over. The color has bled out of Vivienne's face, her skin the color of bone and her eyes like deep pools of crude oil, and her mouth has become a firm line. Her fear energy wing hasn't vanished—quite the opposite, in fact. As Ruby watches, the wing grows and darkens. Then a second wing appears, black and shot through with purple veins. A third. A fourth. Six wings, which unfurl in a burst of darkness.

God. Loki's "better offer" wasn't from Ramisiel. That wasn't the deal he made.

"Ruby Killingsworth, Queen of Goblins," Vivienne says, but it's barely her own voice. "For your efforts, you may go, and live out your life. What remains of it. We will spare you this once."

"Vivienne," Ruby says again, but it's too late. She bites her tongue. "Azazel."

"Yes," Lady Vengeance says. "This tower is our throne. This world will be ours."

"Not fucking likely—"

"Leave," Lady Vengeance says, the voice even darker and less hers. "Unless you wish to join us. Fill that void in your psychopath's heart with *us*."

Ruby wants to snark. Wants to deny her. But in that moment ...

She turns and hurries away, hands trembling.

~

It is only when Ruby gets back to the mansion that she realizes how bad the shaking has gotten. She gets out of the car all on her own, telling the chauffeur not to bother. She hadn't wanted the help to see her upset, but now she's having trouble remembering how to work her own front door. What Vivienne said to her in the tower was hardly the worst thing anyone has ever said to her, but somehow, she can't get those words out of her head. She hears them over and over, echoing in that voice that wasn't quite Vivienne, but was also *definitely* Lady Vengeance.

The door opens from within—she hadn't thought to call off the butler before arriving—and she stumbles into the vestibule. She sheds her bag somewhere, but it hardly seems to matter. She heads for the kitchen, and it's only when she's struggling to open the second bottle of Pinot Grigio that she realizes why.

Maybe there's something to this alcoholism thing after all.

But no matter how much wine Ruby drinks, she can't get Vivienne's face and distorted voice out of her head.

Unless you wish to join us.

At some point, she picks up her StarPhone. She stares at it for a long, long time, trying to fight against the understanding of what she needs to do. She, a woman of unfathomable will, can't defeat her own pragmatism. Unstoppable force meets immovable object.

The line picks up. There's a slight pause.

"Ruby?"

All that work to brace herself, all blown away by just that word, by the sweetness in the voice, by the fact she'd gotten through at all—she'd have bet even money he'd blocked her number. She hadn't realized how much of a wreck she was, but now she's aware that her face is damp, and that she's the one crying.

Not, of course, that she can let him know that.

"Jaccob, I—" She can't say it. She can't let him know what a failure she's become. "Something's happened," she manages after a moment. "I need ... I think we need you."

ROUND SIX: LAST CALL

This is it.

As she steps out of the town car, Ruby takes a deep, steadying breath.

Or at least, that's what it's supposed to be. She takes in as much air as she can without dissolving into a coughing fit and blows it out slowly. Her heart is still racing a mile a minute.

The setting doesn't help. It's just after 2 p.m., but ever since the car came within two blocks of Starcom Plaza, it has grown increasingly dark. The buildings look old, decayed and crumbling, like something from two centuries ago. The few people out on the street scurry out of the way, coughing or cursing. The sun has become a bloody blot in the clouded sky.

The evil in this place spreads like an infection. It's only been a couple days, and already Azazel has claimed two city blocks. Even as Ruby watches, the demon's corruption creeps along the streets and sidewalks, making plants wither, lights flicker, and insects skitter from shadow to shadow.

Did she feel like this the first time she met Loki? When she faced Jaccob that last, horrible night? When she first unlocked the stone?

She's not sure she's ever felt quite this anxious.

"Psychopaths," she assures herself, and not for the first time, "don't feel anxious. That's what makes them psychopaths."

That observation, from some British writer of her distant acquaintance, has always comforted Ruby. It's not that she doesn't have feelings or doubts—indeed, some days, she's nothing *but* the latter. But she learned very early on that exposing how she really feels, opening herself up, sharing her real thoughts—all of that leaves her vulnerable. When she was young and stupid, enough people stepped on her hard enough that she decided to do the stepping from then on, thank you very much. She wove wards and shields around her heart, which had already grown enough scar tissue, it should have been impenetrable anyway.

But this ...

This really should be someone else's job, but she's the one who's here, against every instinct screaming at her to run the other way.

Ruby shakes her head. "You're a damn fool, Ginger."

The doors to the barren tower are a splintered mess: shattered, stained glass and filigree busted away in the few instances the brass faces hadn't been ripped from their frames altogether. The glass in the once-majestic front doors hangs in limp spider webs of destruction. Ruby steps gingerly inside, her magic crackling around her.

If the flagship store was a moldering mess beneath Ramisiel's occupation, it has become a graveyard under the new management. The screens hang limply on the walls, cracked and lifeless. Every plant—including Ramisiel's roots that had ripped through the walls and ceiling—has become a withered husk, or the mere suggestion of a wispy skeleton, and crumbles to dust at the slight touch or even the whiff of a breeze. The floors are covered with a thick layer of dust, muddling the distinction between the white marble and crimson carpets. Cracks run through the walls, and a foul smell permeates the place, something between mold and overcooked barbecue.

"You return," Azazel says, in that voice that's almost Vivienne's but not quite. Ruby isn't sure whether her ears are picking up the sound or it's in her head. "You could not come to terms with your own weakness, and it has brought you, inevitably, back to me."

The demon's magic spreads around her like a muggy fog, unseen but palpable. It slows her, as though she's wading through water, but at least that's all it does.

Ruby spun numerous wards around herself today. She's wearing several layers of invisible magical armor and a jeweled fetish on a silver chain around her waist. Her body may be walking into mortal danger, but her magic is protected like it's never been. She's as steeled for this as it's possible to be.

"There is nothing for you here, Ruby Killingsworth," the demon says. "Nothing but death."

"Is that so?" Slowly, Ruby makes her way toward the elevators.

The demon laughs with Vivienne's laugh, but far worse. Being on the receiving end of that sharp laughter hurts more than Ruby could have expected.

"What power is there in that aging sack of loose flesh?" Azazel asks. "Feel the skin of your face. See the blood under your fingernails. You are dying already."

"Oh, darling," she says, sounding far more confident than she feels. "If you want to hurt my feelings, you're going to have to do better than that."

"*Ruby.*" The voice sounds again, but it's a different voice: Chet Manderly, captain of the football team at her old high school. She hasn't heard that voice in twenty-five years or more, but she recognizes it instantly. And suddenly all those weird, squishy feelings are back.

"Ruby, babe, don't make this weird." Chet's face appears on one of the monitors, young and vibrant and handsome in that All-American way. "Who would date a loser freshman who puts out on the first date? But we can hit the locker room if you're *that* hungry for it—"

He smiles insufferably, in just that way she isn't sure whether she remembers or imagines.

"Oh, come now," Ruby says. "I feel like you're not even trying. Vivienne can get meaner than that just trying to turn me on." Ruby pushes the button to call the elevator, which lights up blood-red. "Why don't you put her back in the driver's seat? I'm sure she'll be so awful to me I'll break right down in tears, and you'll have the run of my building for just a little longer."

Suddenly every screen in the room lights up with static that resolves into Vivienne's face, her eyes smeared with black and purple shadow. It's the post-sex look, and it makes Ruby's heart leap. She speaks like she's being interviewed. No ... it's pillow talk.

"I swear, Jaccob," Vivienne says. "I just don't see what you ever saw in that psycho. She's like a walking wound, but she doesn't even realize she's bleeding. So much perfume she thinks it can conceal the rotting smell. How sad is that." She smiles alluringly.

"Come fuck me already, so I can get the taste of her out of my mouth."

Oof.

"Sticks and stones," Ruby says, then mentally runs through every word of profanity she knows.

She has to stay focused on the larger situation. The demon's magic is strong. Each time it brushes against her personal wards, she feels them beginning to erode like gloss paint exposed to turpentine.

But her magic can fix itself, especially here, especially in this place where she'd broken the first ground and laid the first stone with her own bare hands, this place where she'd spun magic into every level, every layer, and received her new powers through the Ritual of the Scrolls. This is *her* place.

In this place, like clings to like, and the magic she carries is as self-healing as it is powerful. In many ways, she's in terrible danger, but in this one way, she is as safe as she's ever been. Azazel has made a big mistake challenging her here.

That's what she keeps telling herself, anyway.

"You're pathetic, you know," Vivienne says. "I only felt sorry for you. Because I have actual feelings. And what did that get me? Shitty sex and eternal servitude. Thanks for nothing."

That didn't sound like Azazel, but Ruby shuts it out.

With the scream of rickety gears, the elevator dings open, glowing orange and red inside as if with flames. Words are written all over the glass inside, with blood or lipstick, she can't quite tell. Some are indecipherable, but others, she can read all too well. They're words she and Vivienne shared, in private, dark moments, entwined, laughing at one another. All of them turned violent. Grotesque. Used to hurt her.

Ruby stiffens her spine. If Azazel wants her dead, he could have done it when she stepped into the tower. No, he wants to torture her as much as he can. To break her, like he broke Vivienne.

But not Ruby Killingsworth. Not here. Not now.

She steps inside the elevator and pushes the button for the corporate floor.

She hears more whispers from Vivienne as the elevator clanks and whines upward, all the little embarrassing endearments and barbs, twisted into depravity and hate. None of it is obviously hurtful, but listening to that banter out of context makes Ruby's teeth grind and her chest feel tight. How does Azazel know any of this, let alone what to use against her? Either he has full run of Vivienne's mind and feelings, or Vivienne is part of it ...

No. She can't believe that. If she starts thinking that way, this is all over.

And she hasn't shot her shot yet.

The elevator reaches its destination, and dings open into the cavernous remains of her formerly gleaming corporate headquarters. She strides through the shredded shell of what once was the center of her kingdom, breathing in the memory of every previous walk through these halls. These are her halls. This is her domain. She is the once and future queen of this place, and she has come to reclaim her throne.

The familiarity of the path from reception to the C-suite is calming, the sound of her heels against the carpet steels her. It steels her, but nothing can prepare her—not really—for the state of her private office when she reaches it.

The place looks like an abandoned, weather-stripped cathedral or the hollowed-out great hall of a gothic castle left to rot on the coast. Gone is the charm and beauty of utility, the simple and elegant lines of furniture and function. Her great imported desk is covered with cobwebs and choked with dust, the papers upon it yellowing and aged. This place is dead.

Most of those papers, she realizes, are pictures of her, full of heedless smiles or knowing smirks, some in extremely scandalous, compromising positions. Ruby knows for a *fact* that no one has photographed her at many of those less-than-flattering angles, and she hasn't been into amateur erotic art for over twenty years, since that phase she doesn't like to think about.

Are these real pictures? Is any of this real? Is the demon already inside her head?

Her defenses seem weak, worn and shabby like clothes washed and dried too many times. Ruby clings to as much of her magic as she can, ready for an assault.

"Vivienne," she says, equal parts a prayer and a challenge.

As though summoned, there she kneels, head down and face hidden behind a stringy mess of black and purple hair. Beneath her worn black leather jacket, her black shirt and jeans have torn and decayed, like everything the demon's influence touches. A black cloak hangs lankly from her shoulders and back, and Ruby realizes those are leathery wings.

The state of Lady Vengeance makes Ruby shiver all over. The word "haggard" seems a paltry and insufficient one for the sickly woman who looms before her, skin the color of clotted cream left in the trunk by accident and posture like a contorted shop manikin gone yellow with age. Her bones scratch at her flesh, as though they might stab through at any moment, and raised tendons stretch so tight under her taut skin as to snap. She looks gaunt and hungry and ... happy. The smile on her face is mad, but it's genuine, and that might be the most terrifying part.

Finally, Lady Vengeance raises her head. Her purple eyeshadow has run down her face in dark, oily tears. She opens her eyes, which have become pools of pitch-blackness—no wine-colored irises or bloodshot whites, only black pupils. The rest of her body may be a wreck, but those eyes are full of hideous life and power, fathomless energy Ruby has only glimpsed a scant few times.

"Ruby Killingsworth," Vivienne says, in a voice not quite hers, but also heartbreakingly hers. "Welcome."

Lady Vengeance raises her clawed hand, and Ruby realizes that the metal has ... grown, or perhaps *spread* is the right word. Like a living mass of flesh, strained and pock-marked black metal tendrils creep up Vivienne's arm and nearly reach her shoulder. It reminds Ruby of the creeping infection of the demon's evil, and that, along with the eyes, snaps her back to reality.

"Vivienne," Ruby says. "You're looking well."

"And you are a terrible liar."

Azazel in Vivienne's body smiles, and her mouth stretches farther than it should. Ruby can practically hear the skin tearing around her chapped lips. Her teeth are yellow and smeared with blood.

"This body." Azazel runs Vivienne's hand down her side. "Vivienne Cain is one of the few who can host me for long. Did you know she welcomes my presence? It is a relief to her. That she no longer has to bear the curse of Adam. Man's original sin."

"I must have skipped that day of Sunday school," Ruby says, taking a cautious step forward. Villainous monologues. Now she sees why the heroic types like them. "Something about defying some bearded old fogey in the sky, am I right?"

"A myth perpetuated by the ignorant and bigoted, but it brushes close to a truth," says Azazel. "There is no god. No divine reality. Only the terrible emptiness of the universe, and lost souls who suffer under the oppression of choice. That is your bondage. Your doom."

"Choice?" Ruby raises an eyebrow. "Last I checked, that's the *opposite* of oppression."

"Do you *feel* liberated?" Azazel points the claw at Ruby, making her pull up short. "You do not know your purpose. Your role. You must choose, and in this way, you are doomed." One of Vivienne's wings rises, black and slashed with purple veins. "You make foolish choices, and thus do you suffer doubt." A second wing rises, then another for each of the demon's denunciations. "Weakness. Regret. Sorrow. Death."

Azazel stands before her in Vivienne's body, its six wings spread wide and pulsing with more magic than Ruby has ever imagined a single entity wielding, let alone held herself. She is incredibly, hopelessly overmatched, and there's no hero to come save the day.

"I appreciate the opinion," Ruby says. "But I have considered the choice to save my friend, and I'm content with it."

"That—" Vivienne's voice cracks and sounds more like herself. She offers Ruby a winsome smile. "That might be the most romantic thing you've said to me, Ginger."

Ruby can tell the demon wants her to think she's gotten her way—wants her to think Vivienne is the one saying these things. But her magic and her intimate familiarity with the woman and her body language tell her that's not the case. But she can get close now, and maybe that's something.

"Don't let it go to your head," she says, smiling down at this Lady Vengeance in a way the real Vivienne might take as foreplay. She's not sure whether the demon will buy friendly banter, but she's able to take another step closer, and that's good.

Behind her, she feels a presence building. Ruby's ears pop as the beast knits itself into existence, growing ever larger until it looms over her shoulder like the most terrifying iteration of a biblically accurate guardian angel she'd been able to come up with when she'd begun the rite of its creation.

A demon of her own design, crafted by combining rites and constructed from magic and will as she sprinkled the ingredients secreted in her sleeve onto the blood-smeared floor. It's only a temporary thing, bound to the space and corporeal for only the time the flowers, clay, blood, and ash lie on the floor together. But it's something—a magical combatant with enough intelligence not to need active control.

And bound by her personal wards to keep a polite distance. That's why she had to move forward; the beast couldn't manifest inside her perimeter.

Know-how trumps talent every day of the week, she remembers telling Vivienne in one of their early conversations. And she meant it. This time she hasn't come counting on someone else's expertise to get the fucking demon out of Vivienne and out of her life. This time she's done the extra research to know how to work this magic herself.

This time she came to slay, and she is not leaving until she is satisfied the damned thing is slain.

If the demon is afraid of the angelic being lurking over Ruby's shoulder, it shows no sign. Vivienne hasn't looked away from her, nor taken any offensive stance. "You are confident," she says. "I admire that about you. But why?"

"Why?" Ruby asks. "Why what?"

"Why oppose me?" Azazel asks. "I know better than to offer you power or influence. You and I are alike. Think of what we could do together."

"Hard pass." Ruby scowls in distaste. "You have something I want. Give it to me."

"No—do not pretend to be one of *them*. Not *you*." Vengeance scoffs. "You, who has everything anyone has ever desired. You, who have riches beyond compare and powers beyond mortal reckoning. You, who has lovers of every shape and size and color and truth. What could you possibly want?"

"I want you," Ruby says. "I want my friend back."

"Friend." Vengeance's voice drips with sarcasm. "Was it my friend who pimped me out to Loki? My friend who tricked me into helping her save this stupid phallic tower? My friend who fed me to

112

Ramisiel—who made me whore myself to Azazel for her own ends? *Again?*"

Her demon roars, and Ruby flinches despite herself. It's only an image, created by her own magic. It can't hurt her. Right?

"*I'm sorry*," she wants to say, because she is, but she doesn't say it. Instead, she stiffens her shoulders. "Demon, you will leave this woman right this moment. You will return her to me and—"

Vengeance cuts her off with the last thing Ruby expected: a fit of laughter. "Is that—is that what you think is going on? Oh, what a fool you are, Ruby Killingsworth."

So speaking, it slashes its clawed hand through the air, the talons rending reality. Beyond and between, Ruby sees a familiar multi-armed demonic creature curled into a ball someplace dark and crackling with purple energy. All around it, she sees images of it, as though it's surrounded by funhouse mirrors.

"Ramisiel," Ruby says. "So Ramisiel is—"

"My bitch, exactly," Vengeance says. "You thought you were abandoning me to die, did you? To become slave to another demon?" Her eyes flare with power. "Never again."

Ruby has to swallow a lump in her throat. "So the danger's past. You can calm down."

"Calm down." Vengeance is abruptly standing in front of her, having moved too fast for Ruby to see. Purple and black flames flicker and wink out along the path she traveled from behind the desk to stand before her. "How dare you. You, who betrayed me. You, who I trusted. What a fool I was."

Abruptly, Ruby finds herself lifted quite unceremoniously off the floor and held aloft by her neck in Vengeance's ungloved hand, and she feels the strain as her body dangles. Vengeance's glimmering purple wings pulse angrily.

"Who's the fool now, Ruby Killingsworth? Who came alone to face me?"

"Who—" Ruby can barely breathe, but she manages to choke out a reply. "Who says I'm alone?"

The windows shatter under a sudden bombardment, and Vengeance breaks eye contact for the faintest of moments. It's just a second—the pivotal second—where a lot has to happen.

First, Jaccob Stevens in his baby blue Stardust outfit, plus some antimagic modifications he added since their last run in, comes swooping through the disintegrating glass storm, blaring bombastic nu-metal on his speakers. Ruby had briefly inquired as to his music choice when he'd announced it during a planning session, and immediately regretted the question when he'd answered: "Because it's cool. Right?" He presents more of a big flashy neon distraction than a genuine threat to a Lord of Hell, but that's his purpose.

At the same time, Ruby looses her conjured angel, whose eyes flash and wings burst in a fluttering torrent of chaos. It smashes into Vengeance's wards like a stormfront, taking just that little extra bit of Azazel's attention, shifting the load of his power just a little more.

Thirdly, the claw—Vengeance's claw—rises suddenly to deflect a .50 caliber bullet fired from Starcom Tower. A Barret M82 recoils slightly at the other end of the bullet's path, sighted from the single glowing red eye of Antonio "The Raven" DeSantes, crouching in his full black combat armor. He wasn't supposed to shoot yet—not until there was no other choice—but is Ruby really surprised? No. Considering that The Raven spent a decade hunting Vivienne with the full intent to assassinate her, she's not even remotely surprised.

While all of that is happening, Ruby focuses on her own spell. She's held the energy all this time, trying very hard not to think about it so as to give away the game, and it has sapped a lot of her strength and will. She's waited for this moment. This tiny sliver of opportunity.

She seizes Vengeance's wrist and pulls her closer until their bodies are pressed together and their faces mere inches apart. Even with all the distractions, the black eyes still shift to Ruby, but it's too late.

"Ugh, *feelings*." Ruby takes a deep breath as though before diving into a sewer, and kisses Vengeance's chapped lips. She tastes of blood and bile and dust.

~

She's standing in a hallway, in a high school with banners, colorful posters, and wood paneling. Beneath the wood, the walls are brick, and the dreary gray outside immediately puts her in mind of an East Coast prep school. The decor is straight out of the 80s, and the longer she looks at it, the worse, more decrepit, less

114

detailed it looks. The textures are rough and generic, like the dull, faded memory of brick and concrete rather than reality. The walls are lined with lockers, some of which are decorated with colorful lettering and stickers she can't read.

It's like a dream, and in the way of dreams, she knows where to go, as though she were just moving that way and paused for a reason she doesn't remember.

"Why are you here?" a voice whispers, barely audible. "This isn't a good place. Not for you. Not for anyone."

Ruby doesn't respond, only starts down the hall. The spell won't last, certainly not long enough for her to waste time bantering with a voice that may or may not be the gothy damsel in distress she's here to save. Ugh, does she *have* to put it like that, even in her head? Vivienne would *not* approve.

"*Will* not," Ruby murmurs. "We are going to have a good laugh about this later. Preferably over some chilled Chablis or at least a good Pinot Grigio."

Ruby's always been adept at convincing herself of just about anything. It almost works now.

Almost.

There's a click, and one of the lockers squeaks open an inch or two. A word is written across the front of the locker in glossy red, and she can actually read this one. Lipstick, paint, or blood, Ruby can't say for sure, but either way, the word "whore" gets the message across.

"Lovely," she mutters. She reaches out to pull the ajar locker open.

It doesn't resemble her own high school locker in most respects. Where she had glossy photos of celebrities, ribbons and medals from music festivals, and neatly stacked folios of sheet music, this locker is a mess of duct-tape wrapped books, black candles, and metal album cover art crudely pulled from cassette tape cases, along with some polyhedral dice whose form and function she recognizes all too well.

"All right, Satanic Panic," she says. "Let's see what you left for me to find here."

Ruby pulls out one book, then another, then starts shoveling the 80s proto-goth trappings out of the locker. Game books, diaries stuffed with bad poetry, a minor spellbook ... It all comes spilling out onto the tiled corridor until Ruby gets to the back of the locker and finds—

Herself.

Ruby blinks at her own face, stretched and distorted. She looks tired, worn, and so, so old. There are wrinkles she distinctly remembers hiding with her makeup that morning—no sense going to fight a demon lord looking anything but your best—and a few she has never seen before. She looks like a strict schoolmarm, rather than a major media magnate. And that: that is the most offensive thing Azazel has done to her so far.

"Now you've done it," she says.

All of a sudden, her hand hurts, and she blinks down at the blood starting to well from her split knuckles. Without even thinking, she'd reached in and punched the mirror, sending a crack through the glass. It is positively unladylike, and she realizes, with a faint smile, that Vivienne is indeed rubbing off on her a little.

She whispers a healing spell, and the wound in her knuckles starts to reknit. Healing isn't her specialty, but since she started spending time with Vivienne, she's glad she reviewed the principles—anything more serious might have posed a problem, but a few busted knuckles she can handle with ease.

The mirror ripples in a very not-glass-like way, and Ruby takes a second look at it. She can still see herself, split in two, but the mirror looks vaguely wet, as if with slime. Less like glass than bone.

She leans back abruptly, startled, as locker after locker flies open, each of them revealing a similar bone-like mirror. On her backside in the middle of the hall, Ruby sees the whole picture: the wall of lockers looks like a set of grinning teeth. In fact, all the windows out into the overcast sky look like grins as well, and the doors yawn like fanged mouths. She's surrounded by mouths.

It is Azazel, and only now does Ruby see him for the being of insatiable hunger that he is. He is every man who has ever leered at her, smiled greedily at her, licked his cruel lips at her. Every one of those mouths seeks to bite her, tear her, swallow her up. Consume all that she is and all she has done, because in the end, she is just a woman, and that is her purpose.

Or so Azazel believes.

Then the mouths start laughing. Jeering laughter, mocking laughter, unhinged laughter, dozens of voices bubbling with mad

116

mirth. It all builds to a deafening, maddening cacophony that makes Ruby cover her ears and stagger. She runs, desperate to escape the awful laughter. She runs amid doors yawning wide to swallow her on all sides, windows that gape at her, fanged maws that whisper her name.

Finally, she sees a door that looks like an actual door, marked with a silhouette in a dress and the word "Lady's." Is that a misspelling, or some kind of clue? And while she has made it a policy to have only gender-neutral bathrooms in her buildings, that symbol activates a deep, old recognition in her, that this place might offer respite from the pursuits of a predatory swarm of male hunger. She shoves through the bathroom door as if into a church that offers sanctuary from an angry mob. The gnashing of teeth and moaning from the corridor seem muted now.

The bathroom is old, worn, and grotty. That's the best word she can come up with for it—the pipes covered with rust and mold, the walls scarred with graffiti and scrawled messages, the mirrors cracked and stained. One of them is missing a long shard. At least they're just mirrors, rather than teeth, and Ruby is glad of that one blessing. The paper towel dispenser is empty, but Ruby wasn't about to risk that sink anyway.

"A girl has to have some standards," she says to no one in particular.

There's a sound—something like an intake of breath—and it draws her eye to the decrepit stalls. The first door is open, revealing a stained toilet that does not bear description. The second door she gingerly taps open, and promptly recoils at the mess in that stall as well.

"Honestly," she says, because snarking is better than vomiting.

Ruby hears it again, and it sounds like a sob. Holding her breath, she knocks on the third and final stall. "V?" she asks.

A sniffling sound is the only reply. Perhaps a compassionate hero might not intrude—might spend hours talking to her through the door—but Ruby isn't that. The stall is locked, of course, but a little flick of magic is enough to deal with that tiny detail. Unlike the others, the door swings outward, because it's the accessible stall, and Ruby looks inside.

"Oh, sweetie," she says.

The girl sitting on the floor beside the toilet is thirteen, maybe fourteen, her body emaciated in the way only an eating disorder can sculpt. Everything about her is a mess, from the smeared, poorly applied black makeup to her torn Hot Topic clothes to the bad dye job, creating a mass of matte black hair with purple streaks that shows bright red at the roots. Her arms, which she holds in front of her face, are covered with cuts and barely clotted blood.

"Vivienne?" Ruby asks.

The girl sobs, then wipes at her eyes, succeeding mostly in smudging new patterns in the mess of makeup on her face. "Who are you, old lady?" she asks, her voice soft and cracking.

"Bless your heart." Ruby holds out a hand. "Come along, dear. We're getting out of here."

The girl makes no move to take her hand. "Can't."

"Sorry, that's not an option."

Ruby seizes the girl by the hand and pulls, but the girl doesn't budge. Instead, she sits staring at her torn-fishnet-wrapped knees pulled up to her chin. She has bruises and scars on her legs, too, and Ruby realizes for the first time why Vivienne has all those tattoos she finds gauche but highly alluring. It makes her chest feel tight.

The floor ripples under her feet, and her skin starts prickling. Cracks spread across the mirror behind her, breaking it into segments. Ruby can hear laughter coming closer, just at the edge of her awareness. Just outside the door.

Teen Vivienne looks up at Ruby with her purple eyes, surrounded by mussed black eyeshadow barely covering up bruises. "What's—what's happening to me?"

Ruby opens her mouth but isn't sure what to say. There's a lot going on, and she understands only so much of it. Her magic is running out, and she can't, for the life of her, think of what to say.

"Ok," she says. "Ok."

Despite her better judgment, as well as every instinct with regard to her not-inexpensive wardrobe, Ruby sits down beside kid Vivienne on the filthy tiles. With some effort, she puts an arm around the girl. She doesn't know what to say, so she says nothing.

The mirror has become a mouth on the wall, leering and babbling threats in languages Ruby doesn't even recognize. She focuses instead on the girl, pulling her into the circle of her protective magic, such as it is. But it's less about the power, and more about the comfort.

The walls disintegrate into a storm of glassy shards, a universe of mirrors and teeth.

As Azazel bears down on them, a storm of angry, demanding male voices, Ruby and teen Vivienne huddle in their little circle of safety.

The hunger is strong, but her magic is stronger. Shored up by Vivienne's deepest desire for peace and rest and powered by her own fierce loathing of the beings who make the sort of cruel demands Azazel seems to be spun from, Ruby is able to push him back.

It's taxing, and it's tough. Sweat pours from her brow and drips uncomfortably down her back. The heat of Azazel's hunger is stifling, making it hard to breathe and harder to concentrate. She clings to the tiny girl beside her, shielding her from the blistering air and the sounds of gnashing teeth and grinding glass.

She breathes into the magic, cooling, calming, muffling. Peace and calm and safety have never been her touchstones, but she knows how to find them in her own space. And this *is* her own space. Grimy washroom and filthy floor notwithstanding, she remembers she is within her tower, the locus of her magic, the place she spun from banal dirt and the ground on which she'd completed the Ritual of the Scrolls.

She holds Vivienne tighter, and tighter still, pushing away everything in this mad not-world until only the sounds of the city, the broken elevator, and the Stardust suit are audible.

When Ruby comes back to herself, she's locked in an embrace with Vivienne—*her* Vivienne, the fully grown woman she'd come here to save. Her conjured angel is gone, torn to ectoplasmic shreds by demonic power. Stardust is crumpled against the wall, coughing, the lights of his armor notably dimmed from abuse. The Raven hangs gasping from Vivienne's claw, where apparently he came to attack but didn't find much success.

"Get out," Ruby orders The Raven, her shaky voice less commanding than she'd been aiming for, but it seems to do the trick.

The Raven nods, his one eye wide with either fear or wonder, Ruby doesn't care which. He manages to escape the grasp of the claw, wiggling out of harm's way only to beat a very hasty retreat, the metal infused with enough magic to know when to let go of an opponent who no longer means you any harm. She's glad for the hours she spent reading up on that claw, on what she might find herself up against if it were to be wielded against her.

Know-how. Trumps. Talent. Every time.

Freed of Azazel's grasp, The Raven leaves without a word. He leaps out the destroyed window and glides off into the night. Ruby is glad to see the back of him.

"You can go, too," she tells Stardust. He doesn't need to be here for what comes next. And what's more, she doesn't want him to be.

But Jaccob doesn't listen. He never does.

"Are you okay?" he asks, flipping up the visor on the Stardust suit as he starts across the room to where Ruby and Vivienne sit in a tangle on the blood-smeared floor.

"I said you can go."

"What——?" It's Vivienne who's talking now. Ruby pushes her hair out of her eyes; and they are her eyes—further proof this is all of and *only* Vivienne sitting here with her. "What—what are you doing?" she asks woozily.

Ruby bites her lip. "You don't want me to say it," she tells Vivienne.

"Well, I do," Stardust says then.

"Jaccob?" Vivienne shakes her head as she looks back and forth between Ruby and Stardust. How had she not realized he was here? "And was——?" She isn't sure. She isn't sure of anything, not even of whether she's going to get a straight answer. But it's worth a try. "Did you bring in Tony?"

"Yeah," Stardust answers her quickly. "And when he didn't stick to the plan, you kinda beat the snot out of him."

"Oh," Vivienne replies. "That's good. You know he never sticks to the plan."

"So I've gathered," Ruby says.

"I'm not going to ask why," Vivienne says. "But I am going to ask—again—what you're both doing here. I only sort of know what's going on, but this ... this I don't understand."

"I think you've gotta say it," Stardust says. He's looking at Ruby in the exact way that caused Vivienne to christen him a Labradork in the first place. It would be cute if it wasn't so infuriating.

"If I say what you want me to say, will you leave then?" Ruby asks, her voice not without venom, but lacking anything either Jaccob or Vivienne would recognize as a threat.

Stardust grins and shrugs, remaining the single most maddening man on the planet.

"Gah! Fine." Ruby draws in a deep breath. "I saved the fucking day. Satisfied?"

"That was beautiful," Vivienne says.

"I feel ill," Ruby says. "This good guy stuff really isn't to my taste."

Then they're kissing.

Jaccob clears his throat, eyebrow raised. "I'll just ... um."

Ruby gives him a dismissive wave.

Vivienne's gesture is much ruder.

"Right," Jaccob says. "You're welcome?"

He flies out through the broken window, but neither watches him go.

They have more important things to do.

EPILOGUE: THE MORNING AFTER

It's early November, and Vivienne wakes up to an unexpected guest yet again.

"How do you keep getting in here? I changed the locks, you know. It was not cheap."

Ruby rolls her eyes, and Vivienne can't help but sigh at the absurdity of her own question. The idea that Ruby Killingsworth, one of the most powerful magic users who's ever crossed her path and one of the richest women in the world, might be foiled by something as mundane as a locked door is, frankly, preposterous.

Vivienne tries again. "All right. How about *why* did you get in here?"

That seems to have an effect on Ruby, who flinches the tiniest bit. "Do you want me to leave?"

"I didn't say that."

"All right." Ruby shrugs her shoulders and wrinkles her nose. "Are you sober?"

Vivienne scowls at her guest. "Why in hell would I be sober?"

"Jesus fuck, Vivienne—it's eight in the morning!"

"Oh, you noticed, did you, Ruby?"

"What happened to Princess? Or Ginger?"

"I am so angry at you."

"For waking you up before noon?"

"That too."

Ruby bites her lip, restraining herself from arguing. "Be that as it may, it's still 8 a.m. on a Tuesday, and you're drunk as a skunk."

"That it is, and that I am." Vivienne concedes the point and buries her head under her pillow, muffling her next words. "Which leads me back to my previous question. Why are you here?"

"I was trying to catch you between benders," Ruby replies, poking at the protective pillow. "Do you need coffee? Sex? A monster to fight? I need you sober."

"Why? To apologize?"

Ruby scoffs. No surprise there. What was a little attempted murder between lovers?

But of course that wasn't what Vivienne was angry about. What she'd had to do wasn't either of their fault, but that didn't make it easy to get past.

"What ... is this a consent thing?" Vivienne asked then, "because that never seemed to be a problem for us before. Boundaries, because magic. Sure. I consent. *Enthusiastically.*"

She meant that to sound flirty, but it comes out more bitter, given the circumstances.

"No, it's—" Ruby sighs and sits down on the bed. "It's not a consent thing. In fact, it's not a sex thing at all. It's a magic thing. Literally." She extends her clenched fist toward Vivienne's face. "A magic *thing.*" With that, she opens her hand, exposing the sparkling item she's held clenched within it, dangling from her fingers.

It's a smooth, round, purple stone—amethyst, by Vivienne's estimation, or alexandrite. Encased in part by a polished swath of black granite, it hangs from a wide-link silver chain of a length that suggests it's meant to be worn as a bracelet.

"What is this?" Vivienne reaches out to take the trinket to examine it further. It reminds her a little of those overpriced engraved-heart toggle bracelets currently in vogue with the Eastside set.

"It's a focus." Ruby clenches and unclenches her fingers. The anxiety is coming off her in waves. "I've anchored a spell in it. The stone holds the spell, but the metal's conductive. As long as you're wearing it, it should muffle the noise."

"You mean the noise of—?" Vivienne's trying to grasp exactly what this thing does. "Wait. You mean—?"

"Other people," Ruby says. "Feelings. That's why I hoped to catch you sober. I thought we could take it out for a test run."

Vivienne slips the bracelet over her hand and admires the way it dangles just so from her wrist. The purple stone starts glowing brighter, absorbing power.

"Wow, you put that on right away," Ruby says. "I expected at least a little more suspicion."

"I said I was angry at you," Vivienne says. "Not that we're not friends."

"Oh." Ruby flushes a little. "I see. We're ... friends. How quaint."

Vivienne realizes that she can feel Ruby, in a way she never has before. If Ruby put up her magical protection, it's not working. Vivienne can smell her anxiety and taste her fear, and beneath it, there comes the heat of a little spark of hope.

"So what you're saying is—" Vivienne burrows out from under the blankets and sits up a little in bed, but she's careful to keep the comforter up over herself. "—I wear this and I won't need to drink so much?"

"That's the hope, anyway. I mean ... that's the idea. There's no way to know how well it's going to work until you've worn it for a while. Using one supernatural toolbox to combat another is ... well—" Ruby shrugs. "It's trial and error."

Sure enough, she's feeling Ruby a little less as she sits there. The gemstone brightens as more energy goes into it. It's not perfect, but Vivienne gets the sense that it will work. Over time, at least. As she adjusts to it.

"But it might work?" Vivienne asks. "It might shut them up?"

"It might. And if it works too well—"

"Too well?" Vivienne interrupts her. "What's too well? I don't hear the fuckers at all anymore and I get to live the rest of my life as a normal person?"

"Yes, that. That and it blocks you from getting what you need from the masses when you need it."

"You mean it could stop me from using their fear?"

"That's what I'm afraid of. Like I said: mixing up arcane energies, it's ... complicated."

"Sure."

"So I made it a little conditional."

"Come again?"

"If you insist—" Ruby smiles. "Anyway, it needs your skin to function."

"So it *is* a sex thing," Vivienne says.

"I mean it." Ruby takes hold of Vivienne's hands insistently. "Push it up over a sleeve or take it off and put it in your pocket, and the flow of power should be interrupted enough to let you get what you need."

"Wow." Vivienne looks closely at the jewel. "That's—wow."

Then she pulls it from her wrist and quite firmly and deliberately hurls the proffered gem across the room, where it bounces off the open hamper and into the pile of clothes haphazardly strewn next to it. The light dims until it resembles a colorful marble.

"What the—?" Ruby blinks. "Jesus, Vivienne. That thing is priceless, and that's before the hours I spent making it do what it does! If you don't want it, you could just—"

Vivienne cuts her off with a kiss before she can say anything else. It surprises Ruby—which is becoming one of Vivienne's favorite things to do, because it's so rare—and for a heartbeat, she doesn't know what to do with her hands. It's really adorable.

Finally, Ruby pulls free of their kiss, both of them gasping a little. "What is this? I bring you what is quite possibly the most powerful magical item these two hands have ever made; you take it from me, put it on like you like it, proceed to throw it across the room like a pair of dirty socks and then ... you kiss me? What the hell?"

Vivienne lays her hands on either side of Ruby's face. "I wanted to feel you."

"You've told me how many times you don't like the feeling of other people—?"

"Other people." Vivienne puts one hand over Ruby's heart. "You are not other people."

She can feel it—the vibrating core of Ruby's heart, bursting through. She sees the moment Ruby finally understands what she's been trying to tell her, and feels all the anxiety disappear, swallowed in a tidal wave of relief and growing ardor. Vivienne leans in for another kiss, and Ruby has no hesitation in meeting her halfway.

Vivienne pulls back and smiles. "The bracelet was really sweet and thoughtful of you. A big romantic gesture."

Ruby wrinkles her nose as she pulls Vivienne closer to her. "Just don't tell anyone, okay? It's thoroughly off-brand for me, and I wouldn't want word getting out."

"Yeah, I think I'll keep this just between us."

They kiss again, deeply and passionately. This time, Ruby remembers what to do with her hands—oh yes, she does—and she's quite agile for eight in the morning. Up until now, Ruby hasn't struck Vivienne as much of a morning person, but this is one subject upon which she doesn't mind being proven wrong.

It must be more than a minute before Vivienne leans away, taking her hands from Ruby's grasp and running them up her back until she can lace her fingers through Ruby's ginger hair.

"It's just nice to know you care," Vivienne says.

"Gah!" Ruby recoils, scowling at Vivienne even as she threads her arms around her waist. "Is that what this is? How do I uninstall it?"

Vivienne laughs and shakes her head. "If I knew that, I wouldn't need your pretty magic bracelet, now would I?"

"You have a point. And it's your pretty magic bracelet now."

"My bracelet, with your magic." Vivienne moves her hands to Ruby's waist and pulls her even closer, on top of her on the bed. "Looks like we make a good team."

"Could be worse."

"Don't say that," Vivienne says. "You care about me."

"Stop it. That's not nice."

"You loooove me."

Ruby shakes her head and snarls. "Oh, fuck *me*."

"Well, since you asked so nicely—"

ACKNOWLEDGEMENTS

This book was an accident, and it was four years in the making. And so the process of acknowledging those who helped it come to fruition is an odd one.

I suppose I should start by thanking Dawn Vogel for both conceptualizing, and subsequently canceling, the anthology that begat the idea to get these two disasters on a page together. And also for helping us turn our beloved mess of a manuscript into a real live book. You are awesome. Never change. Also, we'll get that draft to you soon, I [kind of] promise!

Next I have to thank my amazing coauthor. Erik, you are the actual best. From your absolutely brilliant story concepts to your clever turns of phrase, to the periodic DMs with some form of "we really ought to finish that story," every interaction with you over these years of co-creating has brought me joy. I am still in awe of the fact *you* were keen to work with *me*. Mind blown. Can't wait for the next one!

To my spouse and my kid: thanks for listening all those times I just couldn't help but to tell you the funny thing I wrote, and for dealing with my absence every time I had to lock myself in a room to hit a deadline. And to Sir Toggle of Waggle: thanks for being the best company a writer can have, you are the goodest boy.

Thank you, Seanan, for being the bestest bestie, for being an understanding, sympathetic ear, a safe shoulder to cry on, a constant source of support, and my supplier of all things whimsical—from strange candy and soda to kitty cuddles.

Thank you to Laura Anne, Elsa, Chris & Sora, and all your kids (both human and furry) for being an amazing circle of creativity and happiness. I have the very best friends and I know it.

Thanks to Jeremy & Nate & Rosemary & the whole Cobalt City family for being so rad and never telling me to stop when I announce a hare-brained plan to break something in our delightful shared world. Y'all are the real Agents of Awesome.

Thanks to Scott James & Lindsey for all the encouragement. And a huge shoutout to Jenn, Raven, and Elizabeth, the Wit 'n' Word crew, for the weekly Zoom check-ins and the general commiseration.

And to all my friends and fans who I only ever see online: Whether or not we've ever met in person, I love all of you. I'm so grateful to have you all there, right on the other side of my screen, across countries and time zones, philosophies and backgrounds, to hold me up, cheer me on, call me in, and keep me accountable. This book would not exist without all y'all.

- Amanda Cherry

ABOUT THE AUTHORS

Amanda Cherry is a Seattle-area queer, disabled nerd who still can't believe people pay her to write stories.

Her debut novel, *Rites & Desires*, was released in 2018, and her sophomore work, *The Dragon Stone Conspiracy*, in 2021. She's had short stories published in the Cobalt City anthologies *Christmas Harder* and *Dragonstorm*, as well as multiple editions of *Mad Scientist Journal* and the queer sci-fi anthology: *Ink*. Amanda was on the writing team for the TTRPG *Acute Paranoia* and is an award-winning screenwriter. Her nonfiction writing has appeared across the web on such sites as ToscheStation.net, Eleven-ThirtyEight.com, and StarTrek.com.

She is a member of SFWA and the Broad Universe Motherboard.

Follow Amanda's geekery and hilarity on Twitter and TikTok @MandaTheGinger and follow her literary journey at www.thegingervillain.com/.

~

Erik Scott de Bie is a speculative fiction writer whose favored genres include fantasy, sci-fi, horror, and superheroes, and especially pieces that mix all of the above. He is also a known quantity in the gaming industry, being the author and/or editor of a number of major releases for *Dungeons & Dragons*, *Iron Kingdoms*, the Cthulhu Mythos, and others. His most recent novel series is The World of Ruin, a post-apocalyptic fantasy like *Game of Thrones* meets *Fallout*, and he is currently writing in a new gaming tie-in setting for Archvillain Games. He lives in Seattle with his wife and their menagerie of pets. Find him online at https://erikscottdebie.com/.

Made in the USA
Monee, IL
25 October 2023

45212680R00077